# London spun arou

She crossed her arms in front of her body protectively. "Why do you think you want to marry me, Tyler? You don't even know me."

Tyler stood up and walked over to where she was standing.

"I know you." He took off his hat and placed it on the rectangular preacher's podium. "I've known you since the moment I saw you."

He put his hands on her upper arms. "No matter how hard you tried to hide from me, I always saw you."

Staring into his eyes, it seemed to London that she could see directly into his soul. He was standing before her, unguarded, baring himself to her, and she could see the goodness in him. She could see beyond the dashing bachelor cowboy exterior to the true man he was inside. And he wanted her, pregnant or not.

\* \* \*

**THE BRANDS OF MONTANA:**
**Wrangling their own happily-ever-afters**

Dear Reader,

Thank you for choosing *High Country Christmas*! I'm very proud to say that this is my fifth Harlequin Special Edition book featuring the Brand family and it's the second book in the Brands of Montana series. I'm thrilled to have another Christmas book this year because I get to have many of my favorite things all wrapped up neatly together in one package: Christmas, romance and Montana. For me, it just doesn't get any better.

It was a pleasure to write Tyler Brand and London Davenport's story with the snowcapped mountains of Montana as their backdrop. Tyler Brand, the middle son and heir to Bent Tree Ranch, has made appearances in *A Baby for Christmas* and *A Match Made in Montana*, so he was long overdue for his own story! Tyler's love interest, London, is also featured in *A Match Made in Montana*. I overlapped the timeline for *A Match Made in Montana* and *High Country Christmas*, so readers can see the same scene in two different books from the perspective of different characters. In *A Match Made in Montana* (Josephine Brand's story), you get a sneak peek into Tyler's romance with London. So be sure to check it out!

As always, I love to hear from Special Edition readers. If you write to me, I promise I'll write'cha back! You can email me through my website, joannasimsromance.com. Or you can email me directly at jsimsromance@live.com.

Happy holidays, awesome Harlequin readers!

*Joanna*

# High Country Christmas

---

## Joanna Sims

HARLEQUIN® SPECIAL EDITION®

Recycling programs
for this product may
not exist in your area.

ISBN-13: 978-0-373-65930-2

High Country Christmas

Copyright © 2015 by Joanna Sims

All rights reserved. Except for use in any review, the reproduction or utilization of this work in whole or in part in any form by any electronic, mechanical or other means, now known or hereafter invented, including xerography, photocopying and recording, or in any information storage or retrieval system, is forbidden without the written permission of the publisher, Harlequin Enterprises Limited, 225 Duncan Mill Road, Don Mills, Ontario M3B 3K9, Canada.

This is a work of fiction. Names, characters, places and incidents are either the product of the author's imagination or are used fictitiously, and any resemblance to actual persons, living or dead, business establishments, events or locales is entirely coincidental.

This edition published by arrangement with Harlequin Books S.A.

For questions and comments about the quality of this book, please contact us at CustomerService@Harlequin.com.

® and TM are trademarks of Harlequin Enterprises Limited or its corporate affiliates. Trademarks indicated with ® are registered in the United States Patent and Trademark Office, the Canadian Intellectual Property Office and in other countries.

**Printed in U.S.A.**

**Joanna Sims** lives in Florida with her awesome husband, Cory, and their three fabulous felines, Sebastian, Chester (aka Tubby) and Ranger. By day, Joanna works as a speech-language pathologist, and by night, she writes contemporary romance for Harlequin Special Edition. Joanna loves to hear from Harlequin readers and invites you to stop by her website for a visit: joannasimsromance.com.

**Books by Joanna Sims**

**Harlequin Special Edition**

***The Brands of Montana***

*A Match Made in Montana*

*Marry Me, Mackenzie!*
*The One He's Been Looking For*
*A Baby for Christmas*

Visit the Author Profile page
at Harlequin.com for more titles.

Dedicated to Gail Chasan...

Thank you for taking a chance,
giving me a shot and making me a better writer.

# Chapter One

At the front door of Tyler Brand's cabin, London Davenport paused to slip off her cowboy boots and tuck them under her arm. There weren't any lights on at the main house, just as there weren't any lights on in the cabin. It was summertime, and life on the Brand family's Montana cattle ranch typically started before sunrise; it appeared that she was the only one foolish enough to be sneaking around after midnight.

*This is crazy.*

That was the loudest thought in her mind when she reached for the doorknob and slowly opened the door. The large open living space of Tyler's rustic log cabin was dimly lit by a night-light in the hallway that led to the small cluster of secondary bedrooms. Tyler's room, the master bedroom, was on the other side of the cabin. And that's where she was heading.

As quietly as she could, she made her way to Tyler's bedroom. Tyler's sister was getting married, and the best man, Logan Wolf, a police officer from San Diego, was bunking in the cabin. The last thing she wanted was to get caught sneaking into Tyler's bedroom like a horny teenage girl. When she reached her destination, she stood in the dark, debating whether or not to even try the door. If it was locked, she would be able to chicken out gracefully and no one would be the wiser. But she did try the door, and the door was unlocked.

Instead of turning around as she knew she should, London slipped into Tyler's bedroom and shut the door behind her. She leaned back against the door, her hands behind her body and her fingers still on the cool doorknob. Tyler was sound asleep on his back, covers kicked off his body, pillows on the floor. His Stetson hung on one of the short bedposts at the foot of the queen-size bed.

"Tyler…" She whispered his name from her spot at the door.

He didn't budge.

"Tyler…"

When he *still* didn't budge, London moved away from the door, toward the bed, and promptly tripped over his boots.

"Ow!" She had to drop her boots on the floor in order to catch herself on the edge of the bed. "Darn it!"

She had managed to stub her toe in the process. It wasn't how she had played this out in her mind, but her exclamation of pain had done the job—he was awake now. Tyler rolled out of bed as if he was under attack, grabbed something off the nightstand and switched on the light.

"Jesus, London…" Tyler lowered the revolver he had aimed at her. "I could've shot you!"

London stopped rubbing her toe and stood upright. "Well, why'd you leave your stupid boots in front of the door for me to trip over?"

"I didn't know you were coming, now did I?"

"You *invited* me!"

"I've invited you a hundred different times, in a hundred different ways, and you've never taken me up on it before."

He had a point. She was embarrassed about her klutzy tumble over his boots and she was taking it out on him. This wasn't the sexy scene she had imagined when she first decided to surprise him with a midnight rendezvous.

"Why don't you put your gun away, cowboy?" She nodded toward the revolver aimed down at the ground. "It's starting to feel more like a hostage crisis and less like a seduction."

When he heard the word *seduction*, Tyler couldn't get the gun out of his hand fast enough. He set the gun back in the nightstand drawer and pulled on a pair of jeans. He felt at a disadvantage standing in front of London in his boxers. He zipped up the fly but didn't bother with the top button or a shirt. He didn't want to risk the chance of London changing her mind while he was stumbling around trying to pull himself together.

"I didn't exactly think this through…" she said, watching him zip up his jeans.

"I'm glad you didn't." Tyler walked over to her. "You wouldn't be here if you had."

London was finally, unbelievably, in his bedroom. Over the years, his father had provided internships to

Montana State University students who were majoring in agriculture or animal sciences. Most had been men, some had been women, but none of them had been like beautiful London Davenport. He had thought about this moment ever since he had first met her. But after she had rebuffed his every attempt to get to know her better, he hadn't really believed that she would ever seek him out. And yet here she was—a Nordic beauty, six feet tall in her bare feet, with thick blond hair that fell all the way to her waist. Her oval face with its prominent cheekbones was scrubbed clean with soap and water. He'd never seen her wear anything more than sunscreen on that beautiful face of hers; makeup couldn't enhance what nature had already blessed her with, anyway. She wasn't girlie or prissy or squeamish; she was athletic and she worked the ranch as though she'd been born to it. And more often than not, she was just as covered in mud and manure as the men. He admired that about her.

"I know this is going to sound like a horrible cliché… but I think this was probably a mistake," she said. "I should go."

And there she was again, right on schedule—the London he recognized all too well. That was her MO: take one small step toward him and ten giant steps away.

Tyler didn't respond to her words with words; instead, he responded with a kiss.

He didn't hesitate or think it over. If he wanted her to stay—and he *wanted* her to stay—he had to bypass that overly analytical brain of hers and go directly to her heart. Her tongue tasted minty as he deepened the kiss. He wanted to kiss her objections away, kiss her doubts away. He had believed for a long time that if she would only let down her guard a little, she would see that they could be amazing together.

Once he started to kiss her, London stopped thinking about leaving and started to enjoy the feeling of being in Tyler's arms. She liked the way he tasted; she liked the way he smelled. She loved the feel of his strong callused hands on her flesh; she loved the feel of his firm, insistent lips as he kissed her as if he was hungry for her. Before today, Tyler had never kissed her. He had tried every tactic possible to get her to date him: joking, flirting and asking her out for dates. But today, in the barn, he'd used a different tactic entirely. During one of her usual explanations about why she couldn't get involved with him, Tyler had grabbed her and kissed her. Midsentence, in the middle of the barn where anyone could see, he'd kissed her. And it wasn't just a little peck. It was a long, deep kiss that had made her a little weak at the knees. *That* had never happened to her before.

It was, by far, the sexiest kiss of her life. A kiss that had managed to unravel her carefully constructed determination not to get involved while she was in Montana. She only had one more semester to go, and then she was heading back to Virginia. It made absolutely no sense to get into a relationship that was destined to end. Especially with a cowboy like Tyler, who planned on spending the rest of his life ranching in Montana.

But then he had kissed her. And that kiss sparked a flame of passion in her that she couldn't seem to extinguish. She had tried for so long to suppress her sexual needs in order to focus entirely on her education that his kiss had opened the floodgate. Years of desire bubbled up to the surface and left her feeling so sexually frustrated by the end of the day that she wanted to scream from it. She'd tried to take care of it herself in shower; she had tried to ignore it until she fell asleep. But the frustration wouldn't *stop*. It just kept building and building and building until she realized that she needed Tyler. He had started this fire; he damn well needed to help her put it out.

Tyler didn't stop kissing London until he heard her make a half pleasurable, half frustrated sound. When he heard that sound and felt her sway toward his body, he suspected that he had changed her mind about leaving.

"I'm glad you're here," he said to her quietly.

"I…" She wasn't sure she could say the same. *Was* she glad that she was here? "…like the way you kiss me."

He smiled at her with his eyes and kissed her again. When his arms encircled her body, she stepped closer to him and returned Tyler's embrace. She closed her eyes, closed out any doubting thoughts, and allowed herself to get lost in the moment. Tyler's lips moved to her neck to drop warm kisses from her earlobe down to her shoulder. He lifted his head and slid his hands down her arms; there was a question mark in his cornflower-blue eyes.

She looked at him directly, with a gaze that never wavered, and lifted her tank top over her head. She dropped it on the floor behind her. Tyler watched her with unabashed appreciation as she unhooked the front clasp of her bra. She slowly slid the straps of her bra off her shoulders and dropped it on the floor next to her tank top. She had wondered if it would be uncomfortable to be undressed in front of Tyler, but it felt completely natural to her. She wasn't embarrassed. She wasn't shy. In fact, the predatory glint in his eyes while he openly admired her naked breasts made her feel sexy and feminine—two feelings she didn't often experience.

She had answered his question with her actions. He needed to know if she had come for more than his kisses, and when she took off her top and her bra, it was all the green light he required. He caught her eye, smiled a lover's smile and reached out to trace the curve of her breasts with his fingertips. London had to close her eyes; it had been such a long time since she had allowed anyone to touch her like this. She wanted to savor every wonderful sensation.

"You are incredibly beautiful, London." Tyler bent his head down to kiss her breast.

The moment she felt his warm mouth on her breast, a thought loop started to play again and again in her mind.

*I need to feel you inside me. I need to feel you inside me. I need to feel you inside me.*

"I need to feel you inside me." London held on to his shoulders and whispered the words aloud.

Tyler lifted his head to study her face, his eyes darkened with desire, and then he easily lifted her into his arms to move her to his bed. Once there, London unbuttoned and unzipped her jeans. She lifted her hips and he helped her disrobe. Now all of her clothes were on the bedroom floor and she was completely naked on his bed.

Tyler couldn't help it; a few seconds passed by and all he could do was stand next to the bed and admire London. She was a golden goddess with long, muscular legs and shapely hips. He had imagined her here, in his bed, many times since they had first met over a year ago.

London sat up directly in front of him, her legs tucked to the side. She hooked her finger on his belt loop and pulled him closer to the bed. Tyler threaded his fingers in her silky hair while he watched her slowly unzip his pants. He stepped back away from the bed; she wanted him to strip off his clothes and he was willing to oblige her.

London silently prayed that God had built Tyler proportionate to his six-four frame. She wasn't a petite woman. Men with smaller equipment had never been able to satisfy her. But the minute he was standing naked in front of her, she stopped worrying. Nature had been very kind to Tyler Brand. There wasn't an ounce of fat on his body; he was a made-in-America cowboy—masculine, beautifully built. With a handsome face to boot.

Tyler grabbed a condom from the nightstand drawer, flipped off the light and joined her in bed. He was surprised that she didn't want a lot of foreplay, but all he cared about was making sure that he pleased her. He gently laid his body on top of hers, chest to breast, and settled between her thighs. When London felt Tyler begin to join their bodies together, she lifted her hips and tried to take more of him.

She stared intensely into his eyes. "I need to feel you inside me..."

"I'm trying to be careful," Tyler said tightly.

He had discovered that many women were too shallow to take all of him. Over the years, he'd learned to be cautious in the beginning to make sure he didn't hurt the woman he was with.

"Tyler. I won't break...you don't have to hold back with me."

With a low groan, Tyler sank the full length of his long shaft into her body. Seated completely within her,

Tyler had to pause to collect himself. It had never felt like this before. He had never been with a woman who had taken him so easily, so completely. She was hot and tight; she was a perfect fit. It was going to take every ounce of his willpower to keep his body under control; he needed to focus entirely on pleasuring her.

London closed her eyes as Tyler slid himself inside her. The feel of his hard shaft was a relief. She locked her legs tightly around Tyler's hips to keep him deep within her and quietly repeated over and over again, "Oh, thank God, oh, thank *God*..."

He started to move inside her, slowly at first, but Tyler soon discovered that London knew her own mind, in and out of bed. She wanted him to love her harder, faster, deeper. She was wild with frustration, as if she had an itch that hadn't been scratched in years. He had never tried so hard to satisfy a woman. He had never tried so hard to stop himself from climaxing.

Tyler stopped moving. "Wait...wait...I need a minute..."

London recognized that expression on his face all too well; she stopped moving to give him a chance to get his body under control. But it was too late.

"Damn it!" Tyler cursed as he pulled back one last time, plunged deep inside her and climaxed.

"I'm sorry..." Tyler dropped his head, closed his eyes and locked his arms so he kept his weight off her. "Damn it..."

London turned her head away from him, near tears from frustration. This was *exactly* why it had been easy for her to avoid sex altogether. Most men couldn't last long enough to get her to orgasm, and more often than not, she was left feeling more sexually frustrated than before she had started.

"You didn't have an orgasm, did you?" Tyler was staring down at her face.

She shook her head. "No."

Tyler cursed again, touched his forehead to hers. "I'm sorry. I held back for as long as I could."

"It's okay." Disappointment and frustration were etched into the features of her pretty face.

"No, it's not." Tyler shook his head. He couldn't believe that he'd just managed to screw up lovemaking with his dream woman.

"It's not your fault, okay?" London looked up at him. "I've always had a hard time…getting there…"

"Then I'll just have to work a little harder next time, won't I?"

"Sure," she agreed. "Next time."

They parted ways. Tyler went into the adjoining bathroom and she started to get dressed.

"Hey…" Tyler reappeared, still naked, holding a washcloth. "Where are you going?"

"We both have busy days tomorrow…"

"Uh-uh. No way." Tyler took her bra out of her hands and led her back to his bed. "That was just the warm-up…"

London let him guide her back down on the mattress, and she let him slip her underwear over her hips. The warmth of a washcloth felt good between her legs, but it felt even better when Tyler replaced the washcloth with the warmth of his mouth.

"Just relax and enjoy," she heard him say. And it didn't take long for Tyler to make her forget that she had intended to leave.

With his hands, Tyler massaged her breast while he kept her aroused with his tongue. She tasted sweet on his lips and Tyler feasted on her delectable pink flower until his body was ready for lovemaking again.

"Don't go anywhere…" He pulled open the nightstand drawer and searched for another condom.

When he didn't find one, he stood up, turned on the light so he could search more quickly.

"You've got to be kidding me…" After another search, he stared at the few items in the drawer.

"What's wrong?" she asked in a tense voice.

He looked at her with a shake of his head. "I think that was the last condom."

London covered her face with her hands to stop herself from screaming at him. She was so off-the-charts frustrated that she almost told him to forget about the condom. But she couldn't get the words out of her mouth.

"Wait…" Tyler went over to his dresser, riffled through the top drawer. Beneath the socks and the underwear, he found what he was looking for.

"Found one," he quickly reassured London. He ripped the package open and put it on. It was too tight, but he didn't care at this point.

"Green?" London was propped on her side, staring at the condom.

"As long as it works, does the color really matter?"

London shook her head; she moved over so he could join her in bed again. He pulled the covers up over their bodies, but when he tried to cover her body with his, she pushed him onto his back playfully. There was an excited spark in her bright blue eyes as climbed on top of him, slipped down onto his erect shaft and moaned gratefully. Tyler groaned loudly and grabbed her hips to push deeper inside her. Moving her hips slowly, London opened her eyes and found Tyler watching her take her pleasure.

She smiled at him in a way she had never smiled at him before. She closed her eyes again, tilted back her head, letting the soft ends of her hair brush across his thighs as she rocked her hips.

"Come on, baby…" Tyler felt her quicken her pace, felt her thigh muscles tighten around him. She was close, so very close.

London's rhythm became frantic; she gripped his tensed biceps, their bodies locked tightly together, until he saw a look of sheer ecstasy wash over her face. She bit her lip hard to stop herself from crying out as her body finally began to shudder. Witnessing the beautiful sight of London's climax, Tyler couldn't hold back any longer. He grabbed her hips, started to thrust harder and deeper, harder and deeper, until he finally exploded inside her for a second time that night.

His heart slamming in his chest from exertion, Tyler opened his eyes to discover that London had been watching him as closely as he had watched her. They started into each other's eyes, both of them flushed with satisfaction.

"So…how was that for you?" he asked after he caught his breath.

London laughed. She leaned down and kissed him lightly. "Incredible!"

She wasn't much of a touchy-feely person. She never had been. But after such intense lovemaking, she *wanted* to be close to Tyler. She snuggled down onto his chest, rested her ear over his strongly beating heart, and let him wrap his arms around her.

"London?"

"Hmm?"

"I think you're a very special person…"

She smiled faintly. "Thank you."

"…and you know that I think we should be more than just friends…"

London didn't want him to finish his sentence. She pushed herself out of his arms and stood up.

Tyler cursed under his breath. "Why isn't it okay for me to say that, London?"

"Because I've already told you that I'm moving back to Virginia after I graduate. You're staying here. I don't understand why we have to keep on having the same pointless conversation." With her back to him, London started to get dressed.

"A woman with a degree in equine science can write her own ticket in Montana."

London yanked on her jeans and quickly slipped on her tank top. "Don't ruin this, Tyler…we had a good time."

Irritated, Tyler rolled to the other side of the bed and stood up. He reached for the condom to pull it off and discard it.

"Oh, *crap*…"

"What?" London spun around.

"The condom broke."

## *Chapter Two*

"What?" She stared disbelievingly at Tyler's back. "No…"

Her normally slow and steady heartbeat started to pound like a jackhammer in her chest. She quickly moved to the other side of the bed, where Tyler was examining the broken green condom. They both stood there silently and studied it. The tip of the condom had blown apart and it was obvious that it hadn't provided any protection at all.

Tyler shook his head in disgust and tossed the condom in the trash. London felt as if she would start cursing if she let herself speak, so she silently pulled on her socks and her boots.

Tyler zipped up his jeans, buttoned them and then turned to her. He looked as sick as she felt.

"That's never happened to me before…" He'd never

come this close to the possibility of a woman being pregnant with his child. He had strong feelings for London, feelings that he doubted she returned. But the *last* thing he wanted right now was the responsibility of a kid.

"Me, neither..." London said in a very quiet, controlled voice. "Where did you even get a green condom?"

Tyler picked up the empty wrapper, crumpled it up in his fist and then threw it in the trash. "Bachelor party."

London's eyebrows lifted in surprise and then dropped as she frowned. "I'm sorry...did you say that you got it at a *bachelor party*? You aren't serious."

"What does it matter where it came from? It broke."

"Trust me..." London glared at him and pulled the wrapper out of the trash. "It matters to me." She studied the wrapper. "Made in India? They have a billion people in India."

"So?"

"India has delicious food, beautiful jewelry, incredible hand-beaded saris...but I seriously doubt that condoms are their strongest export!"

London turned the wrapper over and checked the date. This time she couldn't stop herself from raising her voice. "It's *expired*, Tyler! Three *years* ago! So even if it *did* have spermicide, which I doubt, it's not any good anyway!"

Tyler looked at the expiration date; she was right. It had expired three years ago, right around the time of the party. "Mystery solved why it broke."

"Ya think?" London snatched the wrapper out of his fingers and threw it back into the trash. She sank down onto the edge of the mattress with her shoulders slumped forward in defeat.

"Really?" She looked up at the ceiling as if she were having a conversation with God. "I have sex with *one guy* in years?"

London dropped her head into her hands, face covered. She shook her head. "I can't be pregnant."

Tyler sat down on the bed next to her. "Hey...I doubt that's going to happen."

She didn't lower her hands from her face. "What makes you say that?"

"Well...for one thing, it's actually a pretty rare event, statistically. *And* the first condom was chock-full of spermicide."

"That's true." She nodded.

"And don't forget...that was my second time, so... there couldn't be that many swimmers in the stream anyway." He saw a hint of a smile in her pretty turquoise-blue eyes. "Besides, I've always suspected that I have really slow and confused sperm. So...the few tadpoles who managed to escape from the green condom—the ones who didn't die by spermicide—are probably swimming the wrong way."

Tyler's attempt to lighten the mood worked. They both laughed for a minute at the image he had just put in their heads.

Tyler put his arm around her shoulders. "Look...I don't think you are going to get pregnant. But if you do...I promise...we'll work it out together."

London's shoulders stiffened beneath the touch of his hand on her skin. She stood up, looked him directly in the eyes. "Like you said...it probably won't happen.

So we may as well just go on living our lives like none of this ever happened."

She was standing only a foot away from him, but he could tell by the expression on her face that she was removed emotionally. She wanted them to pretend that they had never made love; she wanted them to erase this night as if it never happened.

"You know…you don't have to leave," Tyler said to her when she was about to open the door. "You could sleep here if you want…"

London looked back at him with a quick shake of her head. "No. I've already stayed too long. Good night."

After she left, Tyler shut off the light and got back into bed. It was strange. It felt as if the past couple of hours were a dream, a figment of his imagination. But he could still smell the scent of her body on his skin, the scent of their lovemaking on his sheets. They had made love…*twice*…and if the stupid green novelty condom hadn't broken, he'd probably still have London in his arms right now. But the condom *had* broken and she was gone.

"Jesus…" Tyler stared up at the ceiling, unable to sleep. "Please don't let her be pregnant."

For the first week after the infamous broken-condom incident, Tyler stopped by the foaling barn every day to check on London. But she was always too busy or too tired to talk. After getting the brush-off for an entire week, Tyler started actively avoiding her. There was a lot of commotion at the ranch now, between his younger sister Jordan's upcoming wedding and the large crew of men who were in the process of moving their great-grandfather's hundred-year-old chapel down the mountain. It was easy for him to stay busy, avoid the foaling barn and try to pretend as if nothing was out of order. But he knew, in his heart, that *everything* was out of order. He needed to find out, one way or the other, if London was pregnant. So, at the end of the third week after they had made love, instead of heading out to the south pasture after breakfast, he went to find London.

After two weeks of not seeing him at all, London was actually glad to see Tyler when he showed up that morning. She'd had enough time to think things over, and now she was ready to talk.

"How's she doing?" Tyler rested his arms on the top wooden plank of the stall gate and leaned forward to get a good look at the pregnant mare.

London ran her hand gently over the mare's side; she stopped occasionally to palpate the mare's heavy, rounded belly.

London finished her examination of the stomach and gave the horse a pat on the neck. "She's doing great. She's put on the right amount of weight. Her measurements are all good. The foal is in a great position. If everything continues like this, I think we'll have a safe birth and a healthy foal right on schedule."

"Mom'll be glad to hear it." Rising Star was his mom's favorite mare.

London unhooked the lead line from the mare's halter and gave her one last affectionate pat. "I've learned to give your mom daily updates."

"That's smart." Tyler slid the latch open and swung the gate toward him for her to walk through.

London nodded and slung the lead line over her shoulder.

"Where're you heading now?" Tyler fell in beside her.

"To the office. I need to jot some things down in Star's file and then I'm expecting the vet soon to take a look at Onyx's leg…it's just not healing right."

Tyler followed her into the barn office. He pulled the door shut behind him to keep their conversation private. "So, you have a few minutes before he gets here?"

London wrote a note in Rising Star's chart and then slipped it back into the file. "A few."

God, she drove him nuts! As usual, she was acting as though she had everything under control in an out-of-control situation. She had to be just as torn up about what happened as he was. Why did she have to be so damned *stoic* all the time?

"I'm sorry I haven't been by lately…" This seemed as good a place to start as any.

"I actually appreciated the space."

Tyler nodded. London liked her space. "I'm at a loss here, London, so you need to help me out. I don't even know how to talk to you anymore."

London looked at him with her typically direct gaze. "I'm late."

He didn't need any clarification. He knew what she was referring to—she'd missed her period.

"Are you regular?"

He'd outgrown his embarrassment with menstruation in his teens due to his two very vocal younger sisters, who had thrived on torturing him with discussions of maxi pads and tampons and cramps. And thanks to them, he also knew that just because a women was late, that didn't necessarily mean she was pregnant.

"Not always." London shook her head.

But Tyler could read the worry in her eyes. She was trying very hard to be casual, but she was concerned.

And that made *him* concerned. She was the least dramatic female he'd ever met.

"So...technically, we could still be in the clear."

"Hopefully." London gave a little shrug with her shoulders. "But I'm not just going to sit around and wait. I'm going to go into town later on and pick up a couple of those early-response pregnancy tests."

"I'll drive you."

She was glad that he offered. She hadn't slept well the past couple of weeks and she felt weary from worry. If he wanted to drive her into town, she would accept the help.

"I should be done here by three."

"Okay. I'll plan on being done around then, too." Tyler checked his watch. "Let's meet at my truck at three-thirty."

The ride into Helena was a quiet one. London didn't have much to say, even about subjects that he knew that she normally liked to talk about. He finally gave up on trying to keep the conversation going and concentrated his attention on the road. Luckily, they both liked listening to country, so he tuned the radio to his favorite station and cranked up the music.

When he pulled the truck into a parking space at the drugstore, London unbuckled her seat belt and said, "You'll wait here."

He didn't know if was a statement or a question, really, but either way, he thought it was best that he wasn't seen shopping for pregnancy tests with London. There were a lot of people in Helena who knew his family, knew him, and a person could never anticipate who might be shopping in the next aisle.

Tyler watched London walk quickly to the store. She had a no-nonsense walk: confident and determined. Her straight, waist-length hair, wet when she had gotten into the truck, had been dried by the wind on their way to Helena. The blunt-cut blond ends danced enticingly just above her small derriere when she walked. The woman was sexy coming and going, as far as he was concerned. This afternoon, she seemed just a little bit more beautiful than usual to him. Maybe he was imagining it, but she looked as though she was glowing. It didn't escape him that he could be looking at the mother of his first child. London Davenport might be, at this very moment, pregnant by him. On the night they had made love, he had prayed that she wasn't pregnant. But today? Right now? His feelings were mixed.

London soon returned carrying a white plastic bag. She climbed into the truck and pulled the door shut. He turned down the radio so they could hear each other talk. Tyler glanced at the full bag.

"How many tests did you buy?"

London opened the bag and pulled out the items one by one. "Two different kinds of pregnancy tests, an economy box of condoms for you..."

London placed the large box of condoms on his leg. He could have protected sex for the next several years without ever running out.

"They were all out of green?" he asked.

"You should take that comedy act on the road," she retorted, but she smiled a small smile as she inventoried the rest of the bag's contents. "Prenatal vitamins and caramels."

"Prenatal vitamins?" Tyler frowned at her. "You didn't take a test while you were in there, did you?"

"No. I got them just in case." She gave him a funny look. "What would it matter if I had, anyway?"

"I want to be there when you take the test. If you are pregnant, I want to find out with you."

London stuffed the items back into the bag. "God help me, you're a romantic, aren't you?"

"My parents have been married for a long time. So, yeah…" he said a little bit defensively. "I do believe that some people get to marry their soul mates."

"Sorry…I can get really cranky when I'm tired. I do think it's nice that you want to be there."

Tyler nodded, accepting her apology. After a minute of silence, he asked her pensively, "Do you think you're pregnant, London?"

"Honestly? My gut says yes. But then again, I've been really stressed-out lately about coming up with tuition money for my last semester. Stress could be making me late."

But, until she took the test, speculation was the best either of them could do. Yet a woman's intuition wasn't something to take lightly. Tyler started the engine but didn't pull out of the parking space. He glanced over at London, who looked back at him curiously.

"We drove all the way into Helena. It seems like a waste for us to just turn right around and head back to the ranch."

"I don't have anything else to do here." London said. "Do you?"

"No. But for the sake of argument…let's just say that you *are* pregnant," he said. "Wouldn't it be nice if I had taken you out to dinner at least once before we become parents together?"

"All right," London agreed.

Surprised, Tyler asked, "Have you ever been to the Silver Steak Company downtown?"

"Uh-uh," she said. "But a steak dinner does seem like an appropriate way to say, 'I'm sorry I got you pregnant with my expired green novelty condom.'"

Tyler smiled as he shifted into gear. "That was funny."

"Well…it's funny now. It might not be so funny after I take the test."

"No…" Tyler pulled out of the parking space. "I think it was funny either way."

Once they were seated in a booth and handed their menus, Tyler took off his cowboy hat.

"Be honest…" Tyler said. "Do I have hat hair?"

London smiled at him. "No. You're fine."

Tyler always looked good. He reminded her of a young Robert Redford—tall, rugged, nice shoulders, charming smile and bright blue eyes. And it didn't matter if he was covered in mud and sweaty from a long day of work or if he was cleaned up, like he was now. He was hands down the best looking man she'd met in Montana. She'd thought that when she first met him a year ago during her junior-year internship at the ranch. And her opinion hadn't changed now that she had taken a summer job at Bent Tree to earn tuition money for her last semester of classes in the fall. Tyler was everything a cowboy should be.

They both decided on sweet teas and steaks. Tyler ordered the filet mignon with caramelized onions for her and the restaurant's famous cowboy coffee steak for himself. While they waited for their main course, they shared a plate of baked brie.

"Oh, sweet baby Jesus…" London said after her first bite of the cheese-filled pastry. "The almond butter should be illegal."

"My mom orders this appetizer every time we come here."

"I love your mom. She's such a cool person." London dipped another piece of baked cheese into a small bowl filled with huckleberry port sauce.

"I know she likes you, too," Tyler said. "You know… I'm sorry about the circumstances, but I'm not sorry that we're finally having our first date."

"I wouldn't really call this a date," she objected.

"What would you call it?"

"Two people eating food at the same table."

"Well…" Tyler took a drink before he continued. "Then I'm happy that you're eating your food at the same table with me."

And he was. He was really happy to finally be sitting across the table from her. He was also proud. They had walked in the restaurant and every male eye was immediately on London. She just drew that kind of attention without even trying. Her height, her hair, her naturally pretty face… She stood out. And it was more than just her beauty that made her noticeable. It was also the self-assured way she carried herself. She wasn't cocky. She was comfortable in her own skin, unpretentious and confident. The looks and the attitude were a potent combination. He could admit to himself that he'd been hooked since the get-go. A lot of women in the area considered him to be a great catch, especially since he was in line to take over Bent Tree Ranch when his father retired. But London had always been able to resist his credentials *and* his cowboy charm. Would she be here with him tonight if they hadn't had to come into town on a separate mission? No. Yet it didn't matter. All that mattered was the fact that she *was* here. It was a place to start.

Their steaks quickly followed the appetizer. London devoured her filet; she hadn't realized how hungry she was until she started to eat. Her plate was spotless, not one caramelized onion or piece of steak left behind. She wiped her mouth with the cloth napkin and then covered her plate with it. She leaned back, hands on her stomach, and groaned.

"I can't believe I just ate that much food. You must think I'm a real piglet."

"I appreciate a woman who isn't afraid to eat in front of me on a date," Tyler said, still working on his steak.

London felt so full and content that she decided just to let the date comment go. "Trust me…when I'm not working like I am on the ranch, I don't dare eat like I just did. All of the women on both sides of my family are overweight. I can't ignore the fact that I've got fat genes."

After their meal, they both agreed that it was time to head back to the ranch. It was another quiet trip from Helena to Bent Tree. They didn't feel like listening to music and they didn't feel like talking. As darkness fell, they were both caught up in their own thoughts. It wasn't until they turned onto Bent Tree's private drive that they both realized the whole ranch was awaiting them at the end of the road.

Tyler pulled over and stopped the truck. "I'm not quite ready to deal with everyone at the ranch. Are you?"

"Actually, no. Not really." London shook her head. "What do you have in mind?"

"If you're up for it, there's something I'd really like to show you."

## Chapter Three

Tyler drove a little farther up the gravel road and then turned right onto a dirt road that was overgrown with brush. Slowly, they made their way through large dips in the road and tall grass until they came upon a locked gate. Tyler left the headlights of the truck on and aimed at the gate. He jumped out of the cab, picked his way through the tall grass and then unlocked the combination lock. It took some brute strength and determination, but Tyler managed to push the gate open wide enough for the truck to drive through.

Once they were safely through the gate, he locked it securely behind them. And then they forged deeper into a part of the ranch she had never seen before. London loved an adventure and it felt as if Tyler was taking her on one now. She loved how dark it was. The only light around them was from the full moon overhead and the truck headlights. She had no idea where they were going and she didn't care. It had been a really long time since she had felt this excited and filled with anticipation.

"I've always wondered where this road went," London said to him.

"I'm taking you to a special spot." He glanced over at her. The light in the cab was dim, but he could see that she was smiling, genuinely smiling, for the first time that day.

They headed farther down the darkened path until they reached a fork in the road. Tyler turned to the left, driving the truck up a steep hill.

"Keep looking up there." Tyler pointed ahead. "You'll see it in a minute."

At the top of the hill, there was a small plateau where Tyler stopped the truck. Straight ahead, two giant cedar trees were growing side by side.

"Do you see it?" he asked.

London leaned forward and squint her eyes. With the help of the headlights, she could see a staircase that led up into the twin cedar trees.

"A tree house?" she asked excitedly.

"That's exactly what it is." Tyler leaned closer to her, opened the glove box and grabbed a flashlight.

"I used to have a tree house when I was a kid! I love them!" When he leaned closer, she caught the scent of his skin. It reminded her of the night that they had made love, and her body naturally responded.

"Me, too." He opened the driver's door and got out. "But I doubt you've seen one like this before. Wait here for me while I check it out. I want to make sure it's safe for you."

London could track his movements as he climbed

the staircase and entered the tree house. A soft yellow glow from a lantern being lit illuminated the interior. This wasn't just a makeshift tree house thrown together by amateurs. This was a tiny house built high up in the cedar trees by expert hands. She couldn't *wait* to get in there and see it for herself.

"Is everything okay?" she asked when he returned. She already had her seat belt off and she was ready to go.

"It's safe. You want to come check it out?"

London pushed the passenger door open. "Just try and stop me!"

The area surrounding the tree house was relatively clear. The root system and the wide canopy created by the ancient trees prevented plants and grass and other trees from growing nearby.

"This is so cool." London followed Tyler up the narrow staircase that wound up the tree to a small deck. "How come I didn't know this was here?"

"It's really only for the family." Tyler opened the front door of the tree house, let her walk through first and then followed.

London felt as if she had walked into a magical world, secretly tucked away, like a hobbit house hidden in a hillside. It was a real house, complete with a small kitchenette, a cozy living room with a fireplace and a spiral staircase leading up to a second floor.

"What do you think?" Tyler made sure the front door was secured.

"It's…" She turned around slowly in a circle, looking up at the tin ceiling. "It's incredible."

"My father had it built for my mom for their fortieth wedding anniversary." Tyler started to open some of the windows to the let the fresh night air stream into the space.

London sat down on the love seat and put one of the pillows on her lap. She breathed in deeply through her nose. "It smells so good in here…just like a cedar closet. If I had this, I'd use it all the time. Do your parents still come here?"

Tyler joined her on the love seat. "Not as often as they used to. If they do come up here, they come here on horseback."

"I'd love to ride horses here…"

"Next time," Tyler promised.

London tossed the pillow to him and left the love seat to explore. "Where does this staircase lead?"

"To the bedroom." Tyler took his hat off and put it on the end table. "A person could live here, if they wanted to. We have running water, electricity, even though the lights in here didn't switch on for me. I think some fuses must need to be replaced. There's a nice shower in the bathroom…a kitchen."

"Is it okay if I go up?" She pointed up the stairs.

He nodded. "I've gotten some of my best sleep up there."

She climbed the spiral staircase, which was designed with tall people like Tyler's dad in mind. She didn't have to hunch her shoulders or duck her head when she reached the loft. There was just enough room in the loft for a queen-size bed and a small nightstand. There were wide windows on every wall, and it made London wonder what it must be like to awaken way up high in the trees. She sat down on the bed with a long sigh. It seemed as if she had been holding in that sigh for years. One of her friends from Montana State was into new age spirituality; she was always talking about the latest book she had discovered and living in the now. She often tried to live in the now, but her focus on the future always overtook her enjoyment of the present moment. She had been working toward her future for so long, working toward returning to her life in Virginia, that she didn't really know how to appreciate now. But in this magical tree house, sitting alone in the loft, nestled in the arms of these two massive cedar trees, she felt peaceful. And she realized that there was nothing wrong with this particular right now. This particular right now was perfect.

London was up in the loft for nearly thirty minutes, alone with her thoughts. Tyler hadn't disturbed her, not once, and she really respected him for it. He was confident enough to give her space. When she came down the stairwell, he was waiting for her, in the same spot on the love seat where she had left him.

"Feel better?" he asked with a knowing look on his handsome face.

She nodded as she sat down next to him. "I wish I didn't have to leave."

"It's funny you should bring that up, because that's what I wanted to talk to you about." Tyler stretched out his legs and crossed his booted ankles. "How about we don't leave? How about we spend the night here?"

London hadn't expected him to say that and she didn't know how to respond.

"Just hear me out…" Tyler understood her hesitation, but he'd thought this through. "When are you planning on taking the pregnancy tests?"

"First thing in the morning."

"That's what I figured. So, wouldn't it be easier if

we took the tests here instead of at the ranch? At least here, we'll have complete privacy."

He continued. "And…I'm not going to say that it wouldn't be nice to share the bed with you. But if you don't want me to, I'll sleep down here."

He was making total sense. She didn't feel comfortable with everyone at the ranch knowing her business. Since Tyler wanted to be present for the test, one of them was going to have to sneak out of the other's room. The last time she'd sneaked somewhere, it had turned out to be a really bad idea.

"You're right. Privacy is important."

If she *was* pregnant, she didn't know what she would choose to do about it. The last thing she wanted, or needed, was to have all of Tyler's family involved.

"And as far as sleeping goes…I'm not going to make you sleep on the floor. We can share the bed."

Tyler went down to the truck to get the bag with the pregnancy tests, and then they both agreed that they should go to bed early. They brushed their teeth using toothpaste they found in the bathroom and their index fingers. Then Tyler grabbed the lantern and they headed up the spiral staircase to the loft. It seemed kind of ridiculous, but London appreciated it when he turned his back to her so she could strip down to her underwear and put on his white undershirt. The cotton T-shirt, snug over her breasts, smelled strongly of Tyler's scent.

"Thanks," she said. "I'm done."

She pulled back the comforter and slid underneath it. She kicked the bottom of the sheets to loosen them and sank back into the pillows. The mattress was soft, just the way she liked it. And the pillows were thick and plush. Now she understood why Tyler had said that he loved to sleep in the loft. The bed was comfortable, and with the cool air coming in through the windows and the sound of the leaves rustling, it was perfect for sleeping soundly. London happily pulled the comforter up under her chin and sighed deeply for the second time that night.

"Comfortable, right?"

"A little slice of heaven." She hadn't felt this comfy since she was a kid.

Tyler, still with his jeans on, lay down on top of the comforter next to her. He pulled the pillows out from beneath his head and dropped them on the floor next to the bed.

"Tyler?"

"Hmm?"

"You don't have to sleep like that. Why don't you get under the covers?"

"Are you sure?"

"We both deserve to get a good night's sleep." She propped herself up on her elbow. "Come on. Take off your jeans and get into bed."

Tyler stripped down to his underwear and joined her in the bed. Part of him had wanted to sleep above the covers for his own sanity. Just the thought of sharing a bed with London had given him a hard-on. The sound of her undressing in the dark had made it worse. He was glad for the dark, so London couldn't see how aroused he was. This wasn't her problem, it was his. So until he went to sleep, he was going to have to deal with his penis being rock hard.

"Good night," Tyler said. Even though he normally slept on his back, he turned on his side, away from her.

London lay on her back for a while, listening to Tyler's steady breathing. It was nice, having a man next to her in bed. She enjoyed the feeling of the heat coming off his skin; she enjoyed the feeling of the weight of his body on the mattress next to her. She'd forgotten how good it felt. But her own body hadn't forgotten. Even though he wasn't touching her, her body was responding to his. That nagging, gnawing desire that had brought her to Tyler's bedroom in the first place was back. Between her thighs, a persistent ache had started. London flopped onto her side, stuffed one of the pillows between her legs and squeezed her eyes shut.

"Are you okay?" Tyler asked. He was still awake.

"Yes." It sounded like a lie because it was a lie.

It didn't matter to her body that it was the wrong thing to do. It didn't matter to her body that the timing was bad. The only thing that her body knew was that it *needed* Tyler's body. She rolled onto her back, sexually frustrated once again. Was it completely wrong to ask Tyler to make love to her again when she knew that she was leaving? Was it wrong to ask Tyler to make love to her again when she knew that he wanted much more from her than she was able to give?

"Tyler?"

He rolled onto his back and waited for her next words to come.

"Did you bring the condoms in from the truck?"

Tyler closed his eyes in silent prayer. He hadn't been able to fall asleep because he still had a raging erection. He needed London in the worst way, but he hadn't wanted to take advantage of the situation.

"They're downstairs." He turned his head to look at her profile. "Do you want me to go get them?"

Quietly, she responded, "Yes."

Tyler got out of bed, quickly retrieved the condoms and returned to the loft. The moon provided just enough light for him to see London sit up to pull his shirt over her head. The sight of London sitting naked in the moonlight, her hair falling over her full, creamy breasts, made him pause just to admire her beauty.

He ripped open the box of condoms while she pulled off her underwear.

"Are you sure you want to do this?" he asked her once he was back in bed.

London took his hand and guided it between her thighs. He had his answer. She needed him as much as he needed her.

"My beautiful London," he said right before he kissed her.

He kissed her lightly and slowly. He didn't want to rush this moment. He wanted to enjoy every second that he had her silky skin next to his. He wanted to enjoy every taste of her lips and the sound of every pleasurable gasp that escaped from them. He teased her with his fingers and his tongue until he was certain that she needed him as much as he needed her. London rolled onto her back, her breathing rapid and shallow. She parted her legs for him and Tyler kissed her deeply as he gradually eased his body into hers.

She pulled her mouth away. "Faster..."

Tyler held himself back. He put his hands on either side of her face so she had to look up at him.

"No." Tonight, he was in control. "This time, we're going to do this my way."

Frustrated and needy, London lifted her hips and tried to take more of him, but he held his body back from her. And no matter how much she protested or squirmed beneath him, he forced her to go at his pace. He filled her body so slowly that it felt like sweet, sweet torture. She realized that she had no choice but to relinquish control, at least temporarily, to him.

Tyler buried his face in her neck as he slowly buried himself inside her body.

"London…" He groaned. "You feel like heaven to me."

Tyler sank the full length of his shaft within her willing body. He hadn't expected it, and neither had she, but London climaxed. She knew that they were far away from prying ears, so she threw her head back and cried out loudly as waves of ecstasy rolled out from her core and fanned out over the rest of her body. Tyler held on to her tightly, held himself steady, and waited for her to ride the waves until their very end. Once she was breathless and clinging to him, Tyler gave her exactly what she had demanded from him in the beginning. He made love to her with more passion than he'd even known he was capable of. He kissed her harder and loved her harder than he had ever loved another woman before. He tried to show her with every inch of his body how much he cared about her. His unrestrained passion drove London to a second orgasm, and at the sound of her joyous cries, Tyler found his own powerful release.

Tyler kissed her lips, her neck, and then slowly eased his body away from hers. Side by side, and on their backs, they let the chilled air cool their skin.

London was the first to speak. "I have to admit… your way has its benefits."

Tyler laughed. "I'm glad you approve."

He was encouraged when she didn't pull her hand back when he reached for it. He knew, in that exact moment, that he loved London. Perhaps he had loved her for a long time and out of self-preservation never admitted it to himself or to her. He loved her. He was *in love* with her. He needed to tell her how he felt...he *would* tell her. But not tonight. Tonight, for the first time in his life, Tyler would sleep with his arms around the woman he loved.

The following morning, the bright sunlight brought with it a heavy dose of reality. London had sprung out of bed, shaken Tyler to awaken him and then rushed downstairs so she could take the pregnancy tests. While she was in the bathroom, Tyler got dressed and waited on the love seat for her. She emerged from the bathroom carrying four tests. She sat down next to him and, one by one, laid the tests out in front of them on the coffee table.

"I feel bad putting pee sticks on your mom's table."

"Don't worry about it." Tyler stared hard at the tests. "There's bleach under the sink. What are we looking for?"

London pointed to each test. "Plus sign, plus sign, two lines, two lines."

"If we see a plus sign or two lines, it will mean that yes, you're pregnant?"

She nodded. "And a negative sign or one line means that I'm *not* pregnant."

"I...think I see a second line on this one..." He leaned forward to get a closer look at one of the tests. "Do you see a second line, too?"

London's body crumpled forward, her hands pressed tightly into her stomach. She didn't want to see it, but she did see a second line. And then, to make matters worse, she saw a plus sign, too. One by one, the tests came back positive. She was pregnant with Tyler Brand's child.

London stared at the four positive tests, her hand over her mouth to stop herself from saying something horrible she might regret later. She wanted to scream and curse and throw something so hard that it would shatter into a thousand pieces. But she couldn't. So she just sat there, staring and knowing that going to Tyler's room that night had been a terrible mistake.

Tyler was staring at the four positive tests as well. Even though he'd known this was a real possibility, he still felt a little bit in shock. And he didn't know what the heck he should say to London. He had the certain feeling that anything he said was going to be wrong.

"You're pregnant," Tyler said robotically.

She looked at him as though he was the dullest nail in the toolbox before she stood up, gathered up the offending tests and shoved them back into the bag.

"I *know*," she snapped at him.

"Do you want to talk about it now?"

"No." She jerked a knot into the top of the bag to make certain that the tests wouldn't fall out when she threw them away. "I don't want to talk about it. We should head back."

Tyler was actually relieved she didn't want to talk. They both needed some time to adjust to the idea. In his family, there was no such thing as pregnancy without marriage. He was just getting used to the idea of being in love for the first time and now he was on track to be a father. Other than his responsibility to ranching, maturity had never really been high on his priority list. Babies and marriage, especially with a woman like London, would take all manner of maturity.

He cleaned up downstairs while London tackled the loft. She quickly made the bed and then sat down on the edge of the mattress to look out the window. The world outside that window was so pretty and peaceful and simple. She placed a hand on her flat stomach.

*Pregnant.*

She quickly began to mentally count out the months in her head. If she kept the baby, she'd still be able to finish her last semester as planned. But she would be *very* pregnant by graduation and she wouldn't be able to hide it.

"What have I done?" London closed her eyes tightly and forced the flood of emotions bubbling up inside her back down. There was no sense getting all weepy. It wouldn't do her a bit of good.

London stood up, plumped the pillows and then headed down the spiral staircase. Tyler was waiting for her; he watched her closely but didn't detect any hint that she might have been crying while she was upstairs. He wasn't all that surprised—she had a stiff-upper-lip attitude. Even so, at the door, he put both hands lightly on her shoulders and waited for her to look at him.

"London…I promise you," he said sincerely. "It's going to be okay."

"That's not a promise you can keep, Tyler."

"Yes, it is." Tyler wrapped his arms tightly around her body, a body that seemed to be trembling from the inside out. "Yes. It is."

## Chapter Four

They returned to the ranch undetected and went their separate ways. They both had jobs to do there, and those jobs weren't going to wait from them to sort out their problems. At the end of his day, Tyler found London in the foaling barn watching over his mother's mare.

"How's she doing?" Tyler asked London quietly.

London glanced at him to let him know that she had heard him before she focused her attention back to Rising Star. She had moved the mare into the foaling stall located at the quieter end of the stable. Horses liked quiet, dimly lit areas to give birth and often waited until nighttime to foal.

London used a calm, quiet voice to answer his question. "She's been showing some pretty strong signs that she's going into labor. Her nipples are thicker and hanging down lower…"

"Any sign of waxing?"

London nodded. Some mares developed a waxy coating on their nipples a couple of days before giving birth, which signaled that they were getting ready to foal. "I was just about to tie up her tail and put down a fresh bed of hay for her."

"I'll grab the hay."

While London set herself to the task of wrapping Rising Star's thick, long tail up and out of the way of the birth canal, Tyler stacked fresh bales of hay outside the stall. They worked in silence, methodically preparing for the birth. Once the tail was wrapped, London left the stall to mix a warm, soapy solution. When she returned with a bucket and sponge, Tyler had already spread the hay around the stall, creating a soft, clean bed for Rising Star.

London quickly washed Rising Star's teats, udder, hind legs and muscular buttocks. Tyler grabbed the feed and water buckets, and then they both left Rising Star alone, in peace. They had done everything they could do to help the mare have a successful birth, but the rest was up to her. All they could do now was wait. Watch and wait.

London slipped into the adjacent stall and sat down in a patch of hay. From her vantage point, she could have her eyes on the pregnant mare without disturbing her. Tyler, to her surprise, joined her in the stall.

"I thought you were going out with your sisters tonight," London whispered to him.

"I never miss a birth at Bent Tree."

Tyler leaned back, one leg stretched out straight, the other one bent. He dropped his worn Stetson onto the ground next to him, rested one arm atop his bent knee and riffled his longish light brown hair. Then he dropped his head backward to rest it on one of the stall's wooden slats and closed his eyes with a long, tired sigh.

London frowned at him. "If you have to stay, you know you have to be quiet, right?"

"You're the one who's talking." Tyler's mouth lifted at the corner, but he didn't open his eyes.

"Shh." She scooted away from him an inch or two. "And quit crowding me."

Tyler crossed his arms over her chest. "Wake me when it's time."

Within minutes of shutting his eyes, Tyler fell asleep sitting upright. She'd never seen anything like it before. But then again, she'd never seen anyone like Tyler Brand before. He was such a hard worker, dedicated to the ranch and his family. Tall. Lean. Cowboy rugged. Cowboy handsome. *And* he made her laugh. It had been a chore to push him away. There had been chemistry between them from the start—he had felt it, and even though she had consistently denied it to his face, she had felt it, too. She just couldn't allow herself to act on the attraction and risk losing focus on her primary goal: get her degree and get back to Virginia ASAP.

For nearly two hours, London sat very still, waiting for the mare to begin labor. As one hour blended into the second, nighttime cooled the air and dimmed the light in the barn. The sounds of the ranch quieted as the last of the ranch workers started their trucks and slammed their doors, their loud voices fading as they drove away. Knowing that mares were known to wait until the stillness of the night to give birth, London had turned on a low-wattage light in the foaling stall so she could still see Rising Star as day transitioned to night.

Tyler was still asleep, it was dark and a little cold, and she had to pee really badly, but she didn't dare move. The slightest noise could stop the mare from starting labor. Fifteen minutes later, her patience paid off. Rising Star began to pace in the stall, making short, tight circles. The mare nipped at her flanks several times before her legs buckled at the knees and she lay down on her side with a moan. Flat on her side, legs extended, her nose nuzzled into the thick bed of hay, Rising Star was in labor.

London hit Tyler on the leg. He stirred but was savvy enough not to make a noise. In a spontaneous show of excitement, they reached for each other's hands, squeezing tightly. This was the moment she had been working toward since she had arrived at Bent Tree. She felt a personal connection with this foal. During her junior-year internship, Tyler's mom had asked her to research bloodlines and select a sire for Rising Star's insemination. When she returned to the ranch to start her summer job, she discovered that Rising Star was pregnant by the sire she had chosen. She felt honored to be the one to care for the mare and her unborn foal in the last stages of a pregnancy. And, now that she knew for certain that Rising Star was in labor, she *had* to be kind to her bladder.

A quick bathroom break, then back to her post. It was so still in the barn, she could hear the sound of Tyler's breathing intermingled with her own. He shifted every once in a while, his arm brushing against hers, but other than that, he was a perfect witness to the beginning of the birth of her foal.

She checked the time on her phone. Rising Star had been down for thirty minutes, but the white amniotic sac hadn't appeared. London had an odd, sick feeling in her gut. She shook her head as she stood up.

"We need to try to get her on her feet," she told Tyler.

Tyler switched on the aisle lights before he followed London into the foaling stall. London had hooked a lead line on the mare's halter and she was talking in a sweet, calming voice to the horse.

"She's having hard contractions," London confirmed. "We should have seen the sac by now. I'm concerned that the foal might be presented wrong."

"Dystocia." Tyler positioned himself at the mare's hindquarters.

London looked at him, surprised. "Yes. Help me get her up."

He had heard about London's ability to stay perfectly cool under pressure, but he'd never witnessed it firsthand. She was calm, confident and certain of every move. She was elegance in motion.

After several attempts, they coaxed the mare to stand.

"Come on, Star..." London led the mare out of the stall. "Let's you and me go for a little walk..."

The three of them walked together, up and down, up and down the long, wide breezeway of the barn. Tyler stayed at the mare's flank to stop her from lying down in the aisle when the contractions started to cause her pain.

"We'll walk her for ten more minutes and then take her back. Hopefully the walking has repositioned the foal and Star will be able to do this on her own," London told him.

Tyler didn't usually take a backseat in the deliveries

on the ranch, but he knew that London had devised a birthing plan with the vet. She needed to run the show. He didn't care about being in charge—all he cared about was seeing Star safely deliver a healthy foal.

"If this doesn't work, then we'll have to call the vet and let him know that he needs to stand by for a possible breech," London continued. "After we get her back in the stall, we'll give this a chance to resolve naturally, but if it doesn't, I'll have to glove up and try to reposition the foal manually and—"

"London," Tyler interrupted her. "The placenta…"

They took Star back to the stall, dimmed the aisle lights and went back to their post. This was the hardest part—remaining still and silent so as not to disturb the birth.

"We have hooves…" Tyler whispered next to her ear.

Excited, she grabbed his arm and squeezed it tightly before she let go. Hooves first meant that the foal had repositioned during their walk and was presented properly now. And it appeared that the fetal sac, a sac that protected the foal once the placenta had broken, was still intact. For a second or two, London closed her eyes and thanked God. But her initial excitement shifted back to concern when Star was pushing and pushing without any success. The mare was already exhausted and the foal wasn't halfway into the world.

"We have to assist. If not, we're going to have a dead foal on our hands."

The mare's neck was drenched with sweat. Tyler knelt down by her head and started to talk to Star, reassuring her, while London slipped on a gown that covered the front of her clothing and gloves that went up well past her elbows.

"All right, girl…" London positioned herself behind the mare. "Looks like we're going to have to get this done together."

London grabbed the foal's spindly legs encased in the slippery fetal sac. She told Tyler, "I'm going to pull with the contractions."

With each pull, the foal came a little bit farther out into the world. "We have a head!"

That was the information Tyler was waiting to hear. The foal's head was where it should have been in a normal presentation. London was patient and persistent, pulling with each strong contraction.

"We have shoulders…" Tyler heard London say. If they could get past the shoulders, they were on the home stretch.

Rising Star made a groaning sound and thrashed her head.

"The foal's out!" London said loudly. She didn't waste time—she cut open the fetal sac that covered the foal's body.

Tyler was at her side. "Is it breathing?"

"Breathing," London confirmed, lifting up the foal's leg. "It's a he."

London peeled off her dirty gown and gloves, disposed of them and then stood in the open doorway of the stall next to Tyler. Neither one of them seemed to have words. They simply stood together and watched the foal wiggling, for the first time, in the hay. Soon, the new mom would regain some of her strength and clean her foal. As much as London wanted to go into the stall, she knew that she needed to let Rising Star bond with her foal without an audience. She'd have plenty of time to bond with the little fellow later.

London wiped the moisture from her eyes and gave a shake of her head to quell the rush of emotion she was feeling while she shut the stall door. Watching a new life come into this world always touched her; no matter how many times she witnessed it, each experience felt like the first time.

Tyler couldn't take his eyes off London. This woman, so strong and determined, was the mother of his first child. He felt *proud* to be standing next to her. He knew, right then, that she was meant to be more than the mother of his child. She was meant to be his wife.

"You did good tonight." He put his arm around her shoulder.

She smiled briefly. "So did you."

She didn't pull away from him, and this gave him reason to hope. They had gone through something here tonight.

"It's two o'clock," London finally said. "You should go and get some rest."

"I never leave the newborns on the first night," he said. When he was a boy of six or seven, they had lost a foal overnight. He'd never forgotten it.

London shook her head. "Neither do I."

"Then we'll both stay."

They each picked a spot in the adjacent stall and prepared to pull an all-nighter. London needed to see Rising Star recover some of her energy and begin to clean her newborn. She needed to see the colt stand up for the first time. Then she could relax. One after another, she tied pieces of hay into knots to give her hands something to do. She had created a little pile of knots when Rising Star finally levered herself upright, found her colt and began to clean him. London smacked Tyler on the leg several times.

Tyler moved closer to her to get a better view of the scene unfolding in the next stall. This was the miracle of life. And, to her amazement, Tyler, whom she had always pinned as a devil-may-care cowboy too shallow to be taken too seriously, *got* it. He was as fascinated with the miracle they were witnessing as she was. She was usually alone with the mare and foal after a birth, and she liked it that way. But Tyler's actions had naturally mirrored her own. He had been completely still—completely quiet. Like her, he wanted to be a witness, not an intruder.

London leaned her body forward, silently rooting for the wobbly legged colt to finally get up on his feet after so many unsuccessful attempts.

*Come on, little fellow. You can do it. Come on...*

Rising Star gave the colt a push with her nose and that push gave the newborn the extra boost he needed to get on his feet.

"Yes!" London whispered, her hand instinctively reaching for Tyler's and squeezing it tightly. She looked over at him—he was in profile and his features were obscured in the low light. But she could see that he was smiling. Rising Star stood up to be with her colt and that was the finale.

In celebration, she found herself hugging Tyler. Hard. He hugged her back, just as hard, and then kissed her on the top of her head.

"This's what I've been waiting for," Tyler finally said in a low voice.

London broke the hug, retrieved a diluted iodine

wash and dabbed it on the spot where the umbilical cord had been attached to reduce the risk of infection. After she applied the iodine, she couldn't stop herself from staring at the perfect little colt. He was black with four white socks. All of these months, she had wondered what the foal would look like, and now she knew. He was a stunner.

"You've got a winner on your hands here, Star," she said to the mare. She loved this colt. She had loved him for months. It was going to be so hard to say goodbye to him when she went back to school. Why couldn't he be hers? London brushed the thought out of her mind with a shake of her head.

Tyler had created a temporary bed out of bales of hay and was waiting for her. The sun would be up in a couple of hours, but she just couldn't bring herself to go back to her room. And it appeared that Tyler was of the same mind.

"Come join me," Tyler said.

"You want me to lie down with you?" London asked, not entirely opposed to the idea.

"I just found out recently that I like sleeping with you better than I like sleeping alone."

She had been stifling one yawn after the other for hours. She was exhausted, so the odds of her falling asleep when she closed her eyes were very high. Why was the thought of falling asleep in Tyler Brand's arms so appealing to her?

"Come join me." Tyler repeated the invitation.

She lay down next to him, rested her head on his shoulder. At first, her body was stiff next to his, but when he grabbed her hand and positioned her arm around his waist, she realized it was ridiculous *not* to relax.

"One of us has to stay awake…" Her eyelids closed.

He rubbed her shoulder. "You rest. I'll take the first watch."

"Okay." She murmured her agreement.

Tyler wrapped her up in his arms and she released a long, tired sigh. He felt her relax with that sigh, which made him smile. Deep, steady breathing followed— Tyler tilted his head to get a look at her face in the dim early-morning light. She had fallen asleep in his arms. And with London sleeping so soundly in his arms, completely trusting him to watch over her, Tyler discovered that he was happier now—hungry, tired and sitting on bales of hay—than he had ever been before.

He had always known that he was going to be a rancher. It was in his blood. But beyond that…beyond what he was going to *do* with his life…he had never known *who* would be at his side when he was handed the reins of Bent Tree. Now he knew. As certain as he was that he belonged to the land of Bent Tree Ranch, he now knew that he belonged with London Davenport… with London and the child growing inside her. They, along with Bent Tree, were his future.

London stood on the threshold of Tyler's cabin, poised to knock. It was impossible not to remember that last time she'd stood at his door…that was the night they had conceived. London knocked on the door quickly; while she waited for him to open the door, she looked around to see if anyone was around to notice her visiting Tyler.

"Hey...I was just about to track you down," Tyler said. He was fresh out of the shower, feet bare. He had nice feet. "Do you want to come in?" he asked. And then he smiled. "Of course you do. That was a stupid question. Why else would you be at my door?"

She stepped inside and he closed the door behind her.

"Is Logan here?" she asked on their way to the kitchen.

"No...I don't expect him back until later. Something to drink?"

"Water. No ice, please." She slipped onto a bench at the breakfast bar.

"We had quite a night, didn't we?" Tyler handed her a glass of water, no ice.

"Thank you..." She accepted the glass. "Yes. We did. Your mom is over the moon about the colt. Who can blame her, right?"

Tyler took a swig from his bottle of beer. "He's a good one.

"I was impressed with you..." he continued with a compliment.

"Thank you." She rested her hands on either side of her glass, glad to have something to do with her hands.

"How are you feeling?" Tyler put his bottle down and put the palms of his hands flat on the kitchen counter.

"A little tired, but other than that...good." He hadn't wasted much time getting straight to the topic they both wanted to discuss.

"Are you feeling...different?"

She shook her head with a small smile. "It's still really early. I don't feel different. Not yet."

"It's still hard for me to wrap my head around the fact

that our baby is growing inside you right now." Tyler stared at her intently. "But the more I think about it, the more I like the idea."

Instead of responding, she took a sip of water.

Tyler came to her side of the counter. "What I'm trying to say to you is that I want our child."

He took her hand in his. "And I want you."

London tugged her fingers free. "I did want to talk about the…pregnancy with you."

"The pregnancy…" Tyler's brows dropped. "That sounds so clinical."

"I'm sorry…" She slid off the stool to put some distance between herself and Tyler. When he was standing so close, it was hard for her to remember to keep her guard up.

"I wanted to tell you that I'm going to continue with the pregnancy."

"It never occurred to me that you wouldn't," Tyler said, surprised.

London's hand naturally went to her abdomen. "And I'm going to back to school. I only have one semester left."

"I was thinking that you could finish your degree after the baby is born…"

"And then I'm going home to Virginia."

They were on opposite ends of the wood breakfast bar. It Tyler a second or two to process what London had just told him. The pregnancy had changed nothing. She was still planning on returning to Virginia and taking his child with her.

"And if I asked you to stay here, on the ranch, as my wife…?"

London saw the pain and confusion in Tyler's deep blue eyes and she regretted that she was the cause of it.

"I'm sorry, Tyler…but no…"

Tyler crossed his arms in front of his body. "No to staying in Montana? No to marrying me…or both?"

"Both…" She whispered the word. "I have to say no to both."

## Chapter Five

She had refused to give him any real explanation for rejecting his offer of marriage. As far as he was concerned, she didn't have a legitimate reason to turn him down. Would having a legitimate reason hurt less? He doubted it.

For the next several weeks, his mind was always occupied, imagining reasons she had to go back to Virginia. Time and time again, he came back to the only logical explanation—it had to be another man. But regardless of that, it occurred to him that she owed him the truth as the father of her unborn child. Instead of heading back to work after lunch, Tyler headed to the foaling barn.

"I thought I'd find you here," Tyler said.

London, who had been admiring the colt Barbara had named Rising Sun, jumped. She had been so enamored with the new baby that she hadn't heard Tyler approaching.

"I have to admit…I'm obsessed." London smiled fondly at the colt before she turned toward Tyler. It was unusual to see him in the foaling barn in the afternoon. "Do you need something?"

"Yes. I need a straight answer from you." Tyler glanced down at her flat abdomen. "I deserve the truth. Are you involved with another man, London? Is that why you turned me down?"

Caught off guard, London was still formulating a response as Tyler took a step closer to her and said in a low, controlled voice, "Because if you're intending for another man to raise my child…to…to take my place as a father…you're going to have a fight on your hands."

London quickly looked around. They had agreed not to speak about the pregnancy until she finished her first trimester. And now Tyler was mugging her in the barn, in broad daylight, demanding answers.

"You think that I would sleep with you when I'm involved with someone else?" she asked in a harsh whisper.

"You've never given me a chance to know who you really are…"

"Well, let me give you a quick overview… I'm not that kind of woman, okay? There isn't another man. That's not why I turned you down." London took a step closer to him. "I turned you down because I have a plan and that plan is to finish my degree and then get back to my life, my *family*, in Virginia."

"Plans change," he stated.

"Not these," she said firmly.

Tyler took a deep, thoughtful breath in through his

nose while he stared at London. Something just wasn't adding up for him. There was always a wall up with her. It was if he was looking at the woman through glass— he could see her, but he couldn't really touch her.

He wanted to shatter that glass wall, but he didn't know how.

Tyler acted on instinct, without thinking it through. He took her face in his hands and kissed her. London kissed him back for a sweet minute before she pulled away.

"We both have work to do, Tyler."

He took a step back, readjusted his hat on his head. "That's right."

When she didn't offer to continue the conversation later, he added in a very quiet, very steady voice, "I'm not going to let you just walk away with my child without a fight unless you have a damn good reason, London. So far, I haven't heard one."

The look in her eyes shifted. She hadn't liked the threat. He hadn't liked issuing one, but he needed her to know his position. She was carrying his child, and for now, she had all the control. But that didn't mean that he would allow her to call all the shots for the long term. "Tonight," London whispered, her eyes skirting around. "Come to my place tonight and we'll talk. *In private.*"

She was angry, and he couldn't allow himself to care. He was willing to put up a fight for his firstborn.

London turned away from him. "Now...you can keep right on standing here, if you want. I'm getting back to work."

That night he prepared himself as if he were going out on a date. Showered, shaved, clean nails, clean jeans... He'd stopped short of putting on cologne. This woman had him plumb confused. He had a hard time concentrating on his work, and he never had trouble concentrating on his work. His work on the ranch was his life. A place where he could escape almost anything...but he couldn't escape London. She was with him wherever he rode, on every job, and he couldn't seem to block her.

Tyler looked at his reflection in the bathroom mirror. His shirt was buttoned up so high that he looked as if he was going on a job interview. He actually always felt as though he was on some sort of strange job interview when he was with London, but he never got the job. Irritated, he started to unbutton his shirt. He yanked it off, threw it on the bed and then pulled on a plain black T-shirt. This wasn't a date. It was a meeting—he needed to remember that.

He headed to the main barn without notice. Working to his advantage was the fact that the members of his family, in one way or another, were occupied with wedding plans for his sister Jordan. His mother was in charge of wedding central in the house, and his father was focused on moving the chapel. He was able to fly below the radar, handle his business with London undetected, and he liked it that way.

London lifted up her plain white T-shirt and looked at her body in profile. She ran her hand over her stomach. It was still completely flat, but she knew that there was a life growing in there. She met her own eyes in the mirror and stared at herself. She already loved this child and would do everything in her power to have a healthy pregnancy. But if she could go back in time, to that night when they had conceived, would she change it? Yes. Yes, she would. She had been trying so hard, for so long, to lead an uncomplicated life, to unravel messy entanglements from her past and live a life free of drama. Why had she gone to Tyler's room that night? *Why?* It was such a stupid, *stupid* decision.

London lowered her shirt when she heard a knock at the door. "Come in…"

Tyler opened the door, entered and then shut the door behind him. She had never had anyone in her small one-bedroom apartment located in the main barn. This was her private space—a place where she could be herself without any judgment.

London tucked her hands into the back pockets of her jeans to give them something to do. "Can I get you something to drink?"

Tyler put his hat down on the café table for two. "No. Thanks. I'm good."

Tyler sat down in one of the chairs at the tiny kitchen table. She joined him at the table, her arms crossed in front of her. This wasn't a conversation she wanted to have.

"I'd rather not waste time with small talk," Tyler said with a grim expression. "If that's all right with you."

She nodded. "I can't live in Montana, Tyler. I know that's what you want. But you need to get that idea out of your head right now. I think it makes sense for me to have full custody, but we can work out a liberal visitation schedule. I'll send pictures…we can video chat every night…but I'm going back to Virginia. That's nonnegotiable."

Tyler circled a scratch on the table with his pointer

finger several times before he tapped the center of the imaginary circle. He looked up at her then.

"It sounds like you've given this a lot of thought."

"Of course. It's my body. My responsibility."

"And you've got it all figured out—"

"I didn't say that—"

Tyler stared at her hard. "—for the both of us."

London didn't answer. She could see by the tension in his jawline and the fire in his eyes that he wasn't done.

"We could have a life here together. I can't be imagining what I feel when we're together. I know you feel it, too, London. I see it in your eyes. But you won't marry me...?"

The question hung in the air between them. When she remained silent, he asked her bluntly. Pointedly. "What's in Virginia, London? If it's not a man...then what is it?"

"My son." London replied. "My son lives in Virginia."

Tyler's finger, which had been making that same circle again and again, stopped. He looked up at the ceiling in thought, shook his head and then brought his eyes back to hers.

"You have a son."

"Yes." Her chin lifted. "I do."

Her twelve-year old son was living with her mom and stepdad while she earned her degree. Her scholarship had taken her so far away from him; she needed to get back to her son.

"You're not with the father." Tyler stated, but there was a question mark hanging on his words.

"No..."

"But…there is a custody agreement." Tyler started to fill in the blanks.

"That's right." London said. "Now you understand why Virginia is a nonnegotiable."

"I was raised to believe that everything is negotiable," he replied thoughtfully.

Tyler had wanted the truth and he had gotten it. He just didn't know what to *do* with it. He was certain that he would find out *why* she had chosen to keep her son a secret in due time. For now, he needed to concentrate on what was directly in front of him: London and his unborn child. So he stood up and held his hand out to London.

"What?" she asked him. Her arms were still crossed and she still had a defiant, frustrated look on her face.

"Come here." He extended his hand farther.

It took her a couple of minutes, but she did take his hand. She stood up, stiff and defensive. Tyler hugged her. It was the only thing that he could think to do at the moment. He had two younger sisters and a sister-in-law whom he adored, and all he could think of was protecting London. Yes, she was a strong, determined woman. But even the strongest woman needed an ally when the going got tough. Tyler rested his chin on top of London's head. He kept on hugging her until he felt her relax in his arms.

"Let's just take this one day at a time," he suggested. Eventually, the right path would reveal itself in time. He believed that.

At the door, Tyler paused. He turned around to look at her. "What's your son's name?"

Surprised, London smiled a small smile. "J.T.…"

"J.T...." Tyler said as if he were trying it on for size as he opened the door. "Good night, London."

"Good night."

She was still staring at the closed door, a bit dazed, when the video chat feature on her phone started to ring. As if he had sensed that she was talking about him, her son, J.T., was calling for their daily talk.

She quickly put a smile on her face before she answered.

"Mom! Look..." J.T. grinned at her.

"You got your braces!" London's stomach tightened. Another milestone missed.

"How do they feel?" she asked as she soaked in the welcome sight of her son's cute face.

"They hurt."

"I remember..." She had had a horrible overbite growing up and her family hadn't had the money for braces until she was a senior in high school.

Before they could continue about the braces, she heard her mom in the background. "What's Gram yelling about now?"

"The kitchen..." J.T. glanced over his shoulder. "I was supposed to do the dishes..."

"You'd better go, then. But call me later so we can talk more."

"She's always mad." J.T. frowned with a glance over his shoulder at the stairs leading from the basement up to the rest of the ranch-style house.

"That's just Gram. It doesn't have anything to do with you. Call me later," she reminded him again. "I love you... I miss you every day."

"I miss you, too." The expression in J.T.'s brown eyes

was somber. "We're still gonna get our own place as soon as you get back, right?"

How many promises had she already broken in his young life? Enough that she could see the skepticism in his face when she replied, "I promise."

They had agreed to keep the pregnancy a secret until the end of the first trimester. It made sense, to both of them, that there was zero payoff for getting everyone stirred up if the pregnancy ended naturally during the least stable trimester. But they had also agreed that once London reached the second trimester, the secret needed to be revealed to both of their families.

"Will your parents be happy?" Tyler asked her.

He was driving her in to Helena for her first doctor's appointment. London had been pensive and quiet for most of the trip. All of his attempts to get a conversation started had failed.

"My mom is a glass-half-empty kind of person, so doubtful. But my stepdad will be, I think. Maybe."

"And J.T.? What will he think?"

London lifted one shoulder. "I'm not sure, really. He's been my only child for twelve years. My ex has two boys with his wife, so J.T. already has two younger half brothers."

She looked out the window, past the pastures in the foreground, to the mountains. "My dad? I know exactly how he'll feel…"

*Angry. Disappointed. Exactly how he felt the last time I got pregnant.*

She had been in her freshman year, on a full basketball scholarship, when she had gotten pregnant. Her father had insisted that she get an abortion, keep her scholarship and get that degree. When she didn't do as he wished, when she lost her scholarship and had to drop out of college to raise her son, her relationship with her father had never been the same.

Did she regret having to drop out of school? Yes. Did she regret having her son? No. Not for one second of one day. But the irony of her situation didn't escape her. Once again, she was going to be a big fat disappointment to the one man whose approval had always mattered the most. After years of fighting her way back into school—after working so hard to earn another scholarship, get back on track and repair her relationship with her father—she had managed to get herself right back into the same mess. She was pregnant *again*.

"What about your parents?" she asked to take her mind off her own family.

"They love grandkids," he said. "But they're old-fashioned."

His mother was going to expect an engagement and his father was going to be livid. Impregnating an intern? Hank Brand was going to hit the roof.

Tyler glanced over at London. He reached for her hand. "It doesn't matter to me how anyone feels. I'm happy about it."

The smile she gave him was halfhearted. He let go of her hand and she immediately pulled it back. If he needed reassurance from her, he wasn't going to get it. In that moment, he was acutely aware of the fact that he could lose London and the child she was carrying. He had lost his grandparents and his brother Daniel. That was enough. He had to figure out a way to make a life in Montana, at Bent Tree Ranch, work for Lon-

don. And the only way to do that was to make Montana
work for her son.

"Here we are." Tyler pulled into the parking lot.

It was a risk for him to come with her. They could
be spotted and their secret blown. But he wanted to be
a part of the pregnancy. It wasn't how he'd planned to
feel. He just did.

London filled out the thick stack of new patient pa-
perwork while Tyler paid the insurance copay.

"Whatever insurance doesn't cover, I'll pay." Tyler
sat down in the chair next to her.

London couldn't believe how much relief and comfort his simple statement had brought her. J.T.'s father,
her high school sweetheart, had been a basketball player
on a full scholarship as well. He had a shot at eventually playing pro ball, and neither of them had wanted
him to miss his chance. Jon had been involved with the
pregnancy from a distance and they had stayed together
until J.T. was three years old.

"Thank you," she said sincerely.

When the nurse called her back, London asked, "Do
you want to come?"

"Is it okay?" Tyler leaned forward to get up. "Are
you sure?"

Tyler shifted in his seat, crossed and uncrossed his
legs, and fidgeted with his hat. He'd never been in an
examination room with a woman before. He'd never actually seen this kind of stirrup until today, and he felt
as if he could have gone his whole life without being
exposed to them.

When the nurse came in to take London's history,
the questions were so intimate that Tyler ducked out of

the room. He waited for the nurse to leave and then he stepped back into the examination room to wait for the doctor with London.

"You didn't have to leave." London was sitting on the examination table in a gown.

"I wanted to give you a little privacy."

"Trust me. All sense of privacy goes out the window during an ob-gyn visit. The worst is yet to come." London raised her eyebrows questioningly. "Are you sure you can stomach it?"

"I'm a rancher." Tyler took his place next to the examination table.

A quick knock on the door ended their conversation. The first part of the doctor's exam was easy enough to handle, but when the stirrups came out, Tyler found himself looking everywhere in the room other than where the doctor was conducting the internal exam. On the opposite wall, directly in his line of sight, was a poster featuring a giant vagina with anatomical labels. He started to read all of the labels to give his eyes something to do, but then he realized that he probably shouldn't be staring at the giant vagina.

He shifted his eyes away from the informative poster and ended up staring directly into London's eyes. She had been watching him and had caught him staring at the poster. The smile on her face and the laughter that he saw in her pretty aquamarine eyes made him smile in return. That brief moment they shared relaxed him a little. But he didn't completely relax until the doctor guided London's feet out of the stirrups and told her that she could get dressed.

When they walked out of the office together and headed to the imaging building next door, Tyler felt as if he was walking next to a woman he had known for years instead of just months. If felt as though they were a genuine couple. And it made him feel proud.

"The look on your face during the exam…priceless," London said while they waited their turn. "You seemed to be pretty fascinated with the artwork."

Tyler knew that the artwork she was referring to was the giant vagina he had been studying. There was a humorous gleam in London's eyes, so he knew she was teasing him. He leaned closer to her and lowered his voice so only she could hear him.

"If you want me to label yours later, I can."

Instead of being offended, London laughed and smacked him playfully on the leg. "Shh."

During her first pregnancy, she had attended her appointments alone. It was strange to have Tyler with her, wanting to be involved in every aspect of this pregnancy. She had let him join her in the room, even though it would be potentially uncomfortable and embarrassing, because she believed that he did have a right as the father of the child. And surprisingly, she hadn't minded him being in the room. In fact, watching him had made her smile. His discomfort had been a little bit of comic relief.

"Ready for round two?" London asked him when her name was called.

"I'm with you." Tyler stood up.

They were led back to another examination room with another examination table. This time, a technician arrived to perform the ultrasound. London was undressed from the waist down again, with a sheet made out of paper over her lap.

London lay back, her feet in the stirrups, her knees

apart beneath the crinkly paper sheet. When the technician began to position the wand for the intravaginal ultrasound, London closed her eyes.

"Just relax…" the technician said encouragingly.

Tyler reached for London's hand, and he was surprised when she didn't reject the comfort.

After a second or two, the technician began to explain what was appearing on the screen. London opened her eyes to stare hard at the monitor.

"Is there a heartbeat?" London asked nervously. "I don't see a heartbeat."

The technician moved the ultrasound wand around and then stopped.

"Right there…there's your baby's heartbeat."

There on the monitor a black steady blip appeared in the grainy gray picture. His baby. He didn't want to take his eyes off it. And he couldn't have known how he would feel once he saw the heartbeat of his first child. Something shifted inside him and he knew that he was forever changed.

"Do you want to keep these as a souvenir?" London handed him the pictures as they left the imaging center.

Tyler took the pictures and examined them closely. His child might look like nothing more than a tiny black dot. But he or she was real.

"What's that expression for?" London asked him with a curious little laugh.

"I want our child, London."

She nodded her head. "I know you do."

"No…" he told her. "I don't think you do. I really want this child, London."

## Chapter Six

The morning after his sister Jordan's wedding, while the rest of his family was occupied with the nuptial aftermath, the main issue on Tyler's mind was discussing the next step with London. According to the calendar, this was the day they officially entered the second trimester of the pregnancy.

He had thought they had experienced a breakthrough of sorts when she allowed him to accompany her into the examination room during her first doctor's appointment. But, if anything, their relationship had regressed. London had put that wall back up to keep him at arm's length. He understood that she was determined to go about her business and stick to her plan of returning to Virginia after graduating in the fall as if she wasn't pregnant with his child. Now that they had finally reached the second trimester, however, ignoring the pregnancy was no longer an option for them.

Tyler pulled on a plain white undershirt and opened his bedroom door. At the same time, his younger sister Josephine, Jordan's twin, was coming through his front door. They met in the kitchen and Tyler poured a cup of coffee for himself. Josephine and Logan, the best man, had started a summer romance at the ranch, and everyone in the family approved of the match. So he wasn't surprised when Josephine looked down the hall in the direction of his guest room, where Logan had been bunking.

"If you're looking for Logan, he's up at the chapel." He took a sip of the hot black coffee.

Josephine had grown into a beautiful, statuesque woman with long blondish-brown hair and a pretty golden hue to her skin. But today she looked pale and tired and worried.

"His bags are packed," Josephine said, looking at the bags stacked in the hall.

"He said he was taking off later today," Tyler told her. "Coffee?"

Josephine shook her head. "Did he tell you where he was going?"

"He didn't tell you he was leaving?" That surprised him. He had assumed that Josephine was the first person Logan told.

His little sister sat down on the saddle bench at his kitchen counter. Now he was beginning to understand why she looked so worried.

"I really screwed up with him, Tyler," she admitted.

"I doubt it's anything fatal. I think he's a really good guy. I'd go talk to him if I were you." He gave his sister the same advice he knew he needed to apply to London—he needed to really sit down and talk with her.

"Yeah…" Josephine slid off the bench. "I guess I will."

Josephine gave him a quick hug and then headed toward the door. She surprised him by making a U-turn and returning to the kitchen.

"I've been so caught up with my own drama that I almost forgot to ask you…" his sister said pointedly, "what exactly did you do to her?"

Tyler put his coffee cup down on the counter. "Whom are you talking about?"

"London. She looked like she was crying the other day…"

"She was?" Tyler was caught off guard by her comment. "Did she tell you why?"

"No…but I do know you're involved with her, Tyler. Don't ask me how I know—I just do, okay? So, what did you do?"

Tyler looked away from her, shook his head in thought before he turned his face back toward his sister.

"She's pregnant."

"Oh…" Josephine stared at him, shocked. "Tyler… that's not good."

Tyler's face took on a stony appearance. "London would agree with you on that point."

"And you don't?" she asked him.

"No. Actually, I don't." Tyler dumped the rest of his coffee into the sink. "I'm in love with her, Jo. I want to marry her and raise our child here on the ranch. But until we've figured this out, I'd appreciate it if you'd keep it to yourself."

Josephine hugged him again and promised to keep the secret.

"I'm having a hard enough time trying to fix my own life," she said. "Trust me…I don't think I'm in a good position to give relationship advice."

Tyler quickly pulled on his boots, shrugged into a button-down shirt and grabbed his hat. He went out the front door and walked purposefully toward the foaling barn. He was surprised to discover that London wasn't there. She was always there at this time of the morning. She was a punctual person who always stuck to her schedule. Concerned, he went to look for her in the main barn. He knocked on the door of her apartment. When she didn't answer his second knock, he had a sick feeling in his gut. He opened the door and entered.

"London?" He noticed a suitcase, half-packed, open on the love seat.

She wasn't in the bedroom, but the bathroom door was shut and he could see that the light was on.

"London?" He knocked on the bathroom door. "Are you okay?"

He heard the toilet flush, heard the faucet turn on. A moment later, London opened the door. Her hair was disheveled, her face ashen. She was wearing an oversize T-shirt and sweatpants. Wordlessly, London went into the bedroom, got into bed and pulled the covers up to her chin.

Tyler knelt down beside the bed. "What's wrong?"

"Morning sickness." London moaned. "I didn't have it at all when I was pregnant before."

"How long has this been going on?" He checked on her every day—she had never mentioned feeling sick.

London licked her dry lips. "For about two weeks. I thought it would pass."

Tyler went to the kitchenette to get her a glass of water. He needed something to do while he calmed himself down. The last thing he wanted to do right now was fight with London. She didn't need to be upset *and* sick at the same time. But he was angry. And hurt. No matter how hard he tried, he couldn't break through with her. London couldn't—wouldn't—trust him.

"Here…you need to drink this." Tyler handed her the glass.

London pushed herself upright. "Thank you."

Tyler sat down on the end of the bed. "I see that you've started to pack your bags."

She nodded as he continued. "London…how do you think that you're going to be able to go back to school feeling like this? You're pregnant. You don't need to be alone right now. You need to be with family."

She stared at him with tears forming in her eyes. He was witnessing the moment that London was coming to terms with her own situation.

He reached for her free hand. "If you don't want to stay here with us, then let me take you back to your family in Virginia. I want you to be healthy and I want the baby to be healthy. Okay?"

She put the half-empty glass on the nightstand, covered her face with her hands and bent forward. She was sobbing, quietly, in front of him and he felt his body freeze. He didn't feel equipped to comfort her. He was about to put his hand on her back when she straightened her body.

"I can't go home." London wiped her tears away with the bedsheet. "I can't go home, *pregnant*, without a degree, without a *job*, barely any money… My mom and my stepfather are already struggling and it's enough that they've been helping with J.T. I deposit the child support into their bank account when I get it, but you know with kids there's always extra…" She wiped fresh tears from her cheeks. "No. I can't go home. Not until I figure all of this out."

Tyler turned his body toward her. "Then you stay here. With me. With my family. We'll take care of you. And once you have the baby, you can finish your degree."

Instead of responding, London waved her hand for him to get out of the way. She flung the covers aside, jumped out of bed and ran to the bathroom. When she returned, Tyler helped her get back into bed. He waited for her to get comfortable before he continued their conversation.

"We've been doing things your way, London. Now it's time for us to do things my way. I'm telling my family about the baby. You're in the second trimester now. You're pregnant with my child and I don't want it to be a secret anymore."

London, who typically had a lot to say about every subject, was unusually quiet this time.

"And you're moving into my guest room today. I want you close so I can keep an eye on you, make sure you're feeling okay. If you aren't better by tomorrow, you're going to the doctor. That's it."

Tyler picked up his hat off the dresser. "What? No argument?"

London tugged the covers up to her chin. She felt exhausted and nauseous and starving all at the same time.

"No." She needed the help and she knew it.

Tyler put his hat on and prepared to leave. "I won't be long. You'll be okay until I get back?"

"I'll be fine," she said. "Are you going to tell your mom that I'm pregnant?"

"Yes. I'm going to tell her now. And then I'll be back to move you into my place. Good thing you already started to pack."

Tyler found his mother working in the study, which had been used as wedding headquarters for the past year. There were boxes and stacks of presents and envelopes all over the room.

"Hi, sweetheart." Barbara Brand smiled fondly at her middle child. "Would you just look at this mess? I don't even know where to start. And of course I just lost my only helper! Your sister has decided to leave with Logan today and is upstairs packing as we speak. I swear I can't keep up with all of you…"

"Mom?"

"Yes, dear?" His mother tucked a platinum strand of hair behind her ear, revealing one of her signature pearl drop earrings.

"You may want to sit down." Tyler took his hat off and put it on the fireplace mantel.

Barbara stopped surveying the mess in the study and spun around to look at her son. He had her full attention now.

"Don't try to soften the blow. Just give it to me straight, Tyler. What now?"

"Are you sure you don't want to sit down?"

"Tyler…" His mother adopted the tone used by mothers universally.

"London's pregnant. I'm the father. Since Logan's

moving out today, I'm going to put London in my spare room because she's been feeling really sick for a couple of weeks."

His mother sat down.

Barbara Brand stared out the window for a minute or two, processing the information he had just shared. When she finally looked at him, her bright blue eyes were filled with disappointment.

"You were right. I did need to sit down for that," she said seriously. "Why, Tyler? Why would you get involved with an intern? You could have any girl in the entire state of Montana…and who am I kidding, you probably have already exhausted the pool around here…but why London? You know your father's rules. The interns are strictly off-limits. Strictly *off-limits!*"

"I didn't set out to get her pregnant, Mom."

Barbara stood up, swiped the air with her hand as if she were trying to wipe the news away. "You shouldn't have been anywhere *near* her, Tyler. Your father is going to hit the roof when he finds out about this."

"I was going to tell him next," Tyler said, still cringing from the sound of his mother's disapproval.

"Oh, no," his mother told him. "You'd better let me tell him this. This kind of news he needs to hear from me. And don't you dare move London into your place until I give you the all clear. Is that understood?"

He was a grown man, but when his mother scolded him the way she was scolding him now, he felt about two inches tall. She could cut him down quick without so much as breaking a sweat.

"First your sister announces she's leaving with Logan, now you?" His mother shook her head in wonder. "What is going on with this day?"

* * *

He didn't hear Hank Brand hit the roof when his mother told him about London, but he felt it in his gut. It was right that his mother broke the news—she had a way with Hank. But he couldn't hide out like a little boy all night. He needed to face his father like a man. Particularly since London, who was feeling better enough to put up a fight, took his mother's side and refused to move to his cabin unless Hank okayed it first. As was his habit, Hank was out at the fire pit, smoking a cigar that he wasn't supposed to be smoking.

"Mind if I join you?" Tyler walked up to the fire pit.

"Have a seat, Tyler."

Tyler sat down on a stump on the other side of the fire pit. They didn't speak for a while. They just sat, in silence, listening to the crackling of the fire and the horses whinnying in the distance.

"Mom told you the news," Tyler finally said.

"She did."

Tyler watched his father over the flames of the fire. Tonight his father seemed older and the lines in his long, tanned face seemed deeper.

"You know…" His father stubbed his cigar out on the log he was sitting on. "Your mother is always telling me that I need to get with the times. Modernize. And I suppose she's got a point. When your sister dropped out of graduate school to pursue painting…when she sold a perfectly good car I had purchased for her and bought that motorcycle…I had to adjust. I didn't understand it, but I had to accept it. Josephine took off with Logan today. Now, don't get me wrong. I like Logan. He's a good man as far as I know. But do I like the idea of them sharing tents and hotel rooms when they aren't married? No. Hell, no, I don't. But, again, I have to accept it."

Hank stabbed at the fire with a crooked stick before he tossed it to the side and looked directly at his son. "But what you've got going on with London… I'm not prepared to accept that."

"Dad…"

Hank interrupted him. "I'm not finished. I don't care how old you are, you aren't mature enough in your brains yet to really know how to treat a woman right. I love you, son. I've given you a good example of how to be a good husband, but up this point you haven't shown me or your mother that you're ready to take on this responsibility. That's why I told you, and every other man on this ranch, that there was a hands-off policy when it came to the interns. These girls are too good to be notches in some cowboy's belt." His father pointed a finger at him. "London's too good to be a notch in your belt, son. And your mother tells me that you want to move her in with you and the two of you aren't married? I'm telling you right now that that's not going to happen. My square isn't going to bend that far."

"I asked her to marry me, Dad. She said no."

"Well, of course she did. She's crazy about you, but she's not crazy. You're not husband material right now."

Tyler kicked dirt into the fire. "London isn't crazy about me, Dad, trust me."

"Like hell she isn't. It's right there for everyone to see whenever she looks at you when she thinks no one is looking. Okay? And you may want to remember that when you're dealing with her."

Neither one of them spoke until Tyler finally said, "I'm sorry, Dad."

"What's done is done." Hank stood up. "But your mother and I happen to think the world of London and we expect you to do right by her."

"I hope you'll be comfortable up here. Josephine changed the sheets before she left, so they're clean. The bathroom is just next door..." Barbara opened up the shutters in the third-story bedroom of the farmhouse to let the afternoon light into the space.

London stood in the doorway, hands gripping the handles of her bags tightly. "I still think that I should stay in the barn. I was comfortable there."

"Nonsense," Barb said firmly. "Now, come on. Bring your bags in here so you can get unpacked."

London didn't plan on arguing with Barb. She respected Tyler's mom and it bothered her that she had let her down.

"Put your things in the drawers, make yourself at home." Barb plumped the pillows before she headed to the door.

In the doorway, Barb paused. "London..."

"Yes?"

"I know Tyler has a lot of growing up to do. But if he wants to woo you properly like he should...give him a chance to win you over."

"Mrs. Brand..." London said. "I'm already pregnant. Isn't it a little too late for wooing?"

"Oh, honey...lesson number one...it's *never* too late."

London had never eaten dinner with the Brand family. She had been invited, but she had never accepted. She had always thought to keep the line clear between her employer and herself, but then she'd sneaked into

Tyler's room and blurred the line beyond recognition. So instead of catching a ride back to Billings with her classmate, as per the plan, she was sitting at the table with Hank, Barb and Tyler. Also present for dinner was Ilsa, the family German shepherd, and Ranger, the family cat.

"All of that activity for months, and now nothing," Barb said after she wiped her mouth with a napkin. "It's so quiet tonight."

Hank nodded his head to acknowledge his wife's comment, but he hadn't said more than ten words during the entire dinner. Like his father, Tyler wasn't much in the mood for conversation. It was one of the most uncomfortable dinners London had ever had, and she was relieved to see Barb finish her meal.

"Did everyone get enough?"

"Yes," London said too quickly, too eagerly, not to be noticed. "Thank you. I'm full." She stood up with her plate in hand. "Let me help you clean up."

"Oh, no, honey... I need something to do with my hands tonight." Barb took her plate. "Why don't you and Tyler go check on Rising Sun? He's been off his feed a little bit, hasn't he?"

Tyler's mom was giving them an opportunity to escape and London took it. Tyler did, too. He left the table, handed his plate to his mom and then followed London out the front door, down the porch stairs into the night.

Halfway to the barn, London started to laugh. "Oh, my stars...that was seriously uncomfortable."

"I felt like we were two teenagers who had just gotten grounded!" Tyler agreed. "They took over before we had a chance to think."

"They're pros. I have to give it to them." London

laughed. It felt good to laugh, even if it was at the ridiculousness of their situation. "They have me sequestered up on the third floor of their house."

"They are trying to make sure that I can't get my hands on you again," Tyler said. "Little do they know that you came to my room, not the other way around!"

London stopped in her tracks. "Don't you dare tell them, Tyler!"

Now Tyler felt like smiling. "I won't tell under one condition..."

"Which is?"

"If you feel up to it, I'd like for you to go for a walk with me tomorrow."

"That's it?"

"I can be bought for cheap." Tyler grinned at her. "Do we have a deal?"

"All right," London said with a shrug. "It's a small price to pay for your silence."

## Chapter Seven

The next morning, it was strange for London to wake up in the Brands' farmhouse. It was still dark when she was awakened with a horrible wave of nausea. She fumbled around, found her way to the door and got to the bathroom just in time. It was an hour before she felt safe to go back to bed. And once she was in bed again, she stayed there until well past sunup.

Tyler's mom was concerned and attentive, not too pushy about insisting that she eat something for breakfast. London always felt famished now, but the constant feeling of nausea deterred her from wanting to eat. So she skipped breakfast and headed out to the barn. Work seemed like the best remedy. If she was going to have all-day morning sickness, she might as well try to do something she loved in order to keep her mind distracted. Once she arrived at the barn, she checked on all of the horses and then let Easy Does It, the mascot mule, out in the paddock. Then she placed a video call to J.T. Her son loved horses, and she had been regularly sending him pictures of Rising Sun ever since the colt was born.

"Can you see him?" London held the phone up so the camera was facing the colt lying down in a pile of fresh hay.

"Yeah—he's big!"

J.T.'s love of animals, particularly his love of horses, had always been a bond between them.

"I know—he's grown so much already. I wish you could be here with me," London said spontaneously, without any agenda. It was how she felt. She wanted her son with her at the ranch. Every experience she had felt a little hollow without J.T.

"I wish you were *here*," J.T. countered. "Hey—aren't you supposed to be back at school?"

London hesitated, her mind searching for something to say that wasn't a direct lie. "Something came up and…"

The sound of her stepfather's voice interrupted the next words that were poised to come out of her mouth.

"Mom—I gotta go. I forgot I was supposed to be helping Pop in the garage."

They said a quick goodbye and just like that, she was off the hook. But trying to skirt the truth with her son was too difficult and it was only going to get harder. Now that she wasn't going to be taking classes in the fall, she needed to use some of the money she had been saving for tuition to buy a plane ticket and fly back to Virginia to see her son.

* * *

Later that day, Tyler joined her near the paddock where Rising Star and her foal were grazing. Rising Sun was trotting in a circle, stubby tail held high, showing off his new sapphire-blue halter.

"He's looking good."

"We started lead training today," London told him.

Tyler had been working all day. He was still wearing his chaps, his sleeves were rolled up to his elbows, and his tanned forearms and neck were gritty with sweat and dirt. In that moment, London felt a feeling in her gut that had nothing to do with nausea and *everything* to do with pure physical attraction. Lust. Tyler was everything a woman would find attractive—tall, masculine, strong features, intense blue eyes and a great smile. Plain and simple—he was sexy. He could easily be a cowboy model on a billboard advertising Stetson hats or Wrangler jeans. She had known on the first day they met that it was going to be hard not to fall for him. Looking at him now, with butterflies in her stomach, she wondered how well she had succeeded in her determination *not* to fall for Tyler Brand.

Tyler tipped his cowboy hat up with one finger, draped his arms over the fence and looked down at her. "How are you feeling today?"

His concern was genuine, and that brought her an odd feeling of security. This time, this pregnancy, maybe she wouldn't feel so alone.

"Really sick," London admitted. "I threw up again this morning. I've been nauseous all day…"

"It's a good thing you decided to stay," Tyler responded.

He was right. It was the best decision. But it was still

hard to see her plans derailed. She didn't have the first clue how she was going to break the news to her family. Now that she had decided to make the trip back to Virginia to break the news to everyone in person, she'd spent the day thinking about *how* to break it gently. What could she possibly say to J.T. to make this right for him? He was counting down on a calendar to the date she was supposed to return home for good. She'd already pushed the date back once.

"The right decision isn't always the easy decision."

"No…" Tyler agreed. "It's not."

After a couple of silent minutes between them, London said. "I'm going to start checking on flights to Virginia. I need to see my son."

Tyler studied London's profile carefully; the thought of her leaving the ranch made his chest feel tight.

Finally, he asked, "Do you need something? Money?"

London shook her head. "No… I've got it covered."

Tyler looked off in the distance and didn't ask the question he was afraid to ask.

*Are you planning on coming back?*

Instead, he asked a safer question. "Are you still up for that walk?"

London, still watching the frolicking colt in the paddock, nodded her head.

They agreed to meet on his front porch in thirty minutes. Tyler wanted to change his clothes, and London wanted to spend a little more time with Rising Sun. London knew that she was avoiding the farmhouse— suddenly, after months of loving to spend time with Barbara, she now felt uncomfortable around Tyler's mom. She used the restroom in the main barn and then headed to Tyler's cabin. When she sat down on the top step of

Tyler's front porch, it was the first time she noticed how tight her jeans were now. With her first pregnancy, she hadn't shown for a long time. Because of her height, she carried extra weight without showing it. But instead of her normally flat stomach, there was a tiny bump filling up the space behind the zipper.

London put her hand on her stomach. She hadn't really come to terms with the fact that she was pregnant. She would love this baby, just as she loved J.T. But did she want to be pregnant right now? No. It was the wrong time, the wrong place, and she couldn't be sure that it wasn't with the wrong man.

Tyler opened the front door. His hair was wet and slicked back from his freshly shaven face.

"I've been looking forward to this all day." Tyler held out his hand to her to help her up.

London stood up and caught a whiff of a new smell. Her body responded quickly and violently. She covered her mouth and bolted up the steps into Tyler's house, ran to the first available bathroom and slammed the door behind her.

He waited just outside the bathroom door. After a couple of minutes, he asked, "Are you okay?"

"Oh, God…" London said. "Something…you're wearing…the smell of it made me sick."

"The only thing I'm wearing is aftershave," he told her through the door.

"That's probably it," London confirmed. "Do you have any mouthwash?"

"I'll get it."

Tyler went to his bathroom, scrubbed his face and neck to get rid of the aftershave, before dumping a brand-new bottle of his favorite aftershave in the trash. He grabbed the mouthwash and delivered it to London.

"Thank you." London cracked the door just wide enough to take the bottle of mouthwash.

He waited for her in the kitchen. When she emerged from the bathroom, holding the bottle of mouthwash in front of her body like a shield, her face was flushed with embarrassment.

"Sorry," she apologized. "That was awful."

"Here…" He handed her a glass of water. "Let's see if you can hold this down."

She took a small sip of water while he watched her closely. Her chronic bouts of sickness worried him.

"I got rid of the aftershave," Tyler told her. "So I shouldn't make you sick now."

London winced and felt the need to apologize again. "I'm sorry."

"Don't be." Tyler put her empty glass in the sink. "I just want you to know that I'm going to do whatever it takes to make things easier for you. Are you still up for a walk?"

London nodded. "I think that fresh air and a little exercise would do me some good."

They walked slowly along the one of the main roads that connected the four quadrants of Bent Tree Ranch. The sudden wave of sickness passed as if it had never happened, and the late-afternoon air and soft sunlight warming her face made her feel better than she had all day. They veered off the main road to hike up the large hill that overlooked the farmhouse, Tyler's cabin and the barns. At times, the hill was steep, and Tyler reached out to take her hand. It was natural to take his hand, to accept his help, in those moments. She had to admit that she enjoyed the feeling of having her hand in his.

"Wow…" London was immediately struck by the beauty of the one-hundred-year-old chapel situated perfectly at the top of the hill.

"That's exactly how I feel every time I come up here." Tyler removed his hat and wiped the sheen of sweat off his forehead before he put his Stetson back on.

"Can we go inside?"

"Sure." Tyler smiled and headed toward the chapel.

"Oh, my stars…" London admired the old curved door with the heavy metal handle and thick hinges. "It's beautiful. I can't believe that they managed to get it down the mountain in one piece."

"I sure as heck didn't think it could be done. But they had it on a new foundation and the exterior fixed up good enough for Jordan to get some wedding pictures taken…" Tyler opened the door for her. "We've still got a ways to go on the inside."

When London stepped inside the chapel she felt as if she had stepped back in time. The inside was cozy and rustic, but there was elegance in the simplicity of the space.

"Your great-grandfather built this, didn't he?"

Tyler sat down on one of the benches that had been handcrafted by his ancestor. "He was a full-time rancher and a part-time preacher."

London ran her hand across one of the stained-glass windows. The world outside looked wobbly and askew when viewed through the heavy leaded blue glass.

"My mom would love these windows. She's so sentimental. She saves absolutely everything. Drives my stepdad nuts. He believes that if you haven't used something in the last six months, you should toss it. My mom's memorabilia is my stepdad's junk. Hard to believe they've managed to stay married for as long as they have."

Tyler watched London explore the chapel. He had a vision of her in a simple white gown, her long hair loose, her belly round with his child.

"I want to marry you in this chapel," he told her.

Surprised, London spun around to look at him. She crossed her arms in front of her body protectively. "Why do you think you want to marry me, Tyler? You don't even know me."

Tyler stood up and walked over to where she was standing.

"I know you now." He took off his hat and placed it on the rectangular preacher's podium.

He put his hands on her upper arms. "No matter how hard you try to hide from me, I can still see you."

Tyler wanted to stare at London. His eyes couldn't seem to get enough of her. Every time he saw her, from the first moment he had ever laid eyes on her, she had made his heart smile. That had never happened to him before. He had met beautiful women—but he'd never met a woman who touched him inside the way London touched him. Yes, she was striking with her thick ice-blond hair and her unusual height. But there was a beauty inside her, an untapped well of goodness, that he had recognized the minute he saw her. That's why he had pursued her. That's why, no matter how many times she rejected him, he had never given up on her. Was this what finding a soul mate felt like? He had to believe that it was.

Staring into his eyes, it seemed to London that she

could see directly into his soul. He was standing before her, unguarded, baring himself to her, and she could see the goodness in him. She could see beyond the dashing bachelor cowboy exterior to the true man he was inside.

"Please, London...tell me that you feel it." Tyler's voice was low, beseeching.

She knew what he was talking about. He was talking about the connection, the invisible electricity that pulled them together. Chemistry.

"I feel it, Tyler."

Tyler stared into her eyes, searching. Finally, his fingers flexed around her arms and he pulled her closer to him.

"Damn it, London... I *knew* there was something between us. Why have you fought me every step of the way?"

"My son," she said simply.

"Why? I don't mind that you have a son."

London took a step back and Tyler's hands slid off her arms. "You don't understand...it's complicated."

Tyler dragged his fingers through his hair several times, frustrated. "I'm right here...*help* me understand."

London sat down on one of the roughly hewn benches with her hand out to support herself, eyes closed.

"I think I need to go lie down," she told him. "I feel dizzy."

His concern for her health, and the health of the baby, took priority. They would have to finish this conversation later. He took her to his cabin, which was closer than the main house, and helped her lie down on the couch. He got her a cool, damp washcloth to put on her forehead and then sat down in an adjacent chair.

"I'm sorry." London still had the washcloth on her forehead and her eyes closed. "Again."

"You don't have to apologize to me," he said. "I just want you and our baby to be healthy."

Her body always had an uncomfortable, visceral response whenever Tyler talked so easily about *their baby*. How could he be so sure of himself when she didn't feel certain of anything? She should be on her way back to school, getting ready to finish her last semester, and then on to graduation and a job that had been lined up for a year. This pregnancy had derailed all of her plans and she felt *angry* about it.

London sat up slowly, swung her legs down and held the tepid washcloth in her hands.

"Why is all of this so easy for you?" she asked him pointedly. "You can't tell me that you were gung-ho to get married and have a kid before *this* happened."

He took the washcloth from her and tossed it in the kitchen sink. He leaned back against the polished wood kitchen counter. "I accept what is. What else should I do? Fight it? What good would that do me? I live today *today* and let tomorrow take care of itself. You should try it."

London stood up, tugged her shirt down. "I'm going to go see if your mom needs some help with dinner."

Tyler caught her hand as she passed by. "If it's complicated, we'll work through it together. You belong on the ranch with me, London. You, me and our child. Together at Bent Tree. You have to know that."

He hadn't mentioned J.T. Was it a simple oversight or a sign? London slipped her fingers free. "I'll see you at dinner."

London loved Bent Tree Ranch. She loved the Brand family. To live on a ranch in Montana, surrounded by snowcapped mountains and a herd of purebred quarter horses? This was her idea of heaven. But J.T.... Would he be happy here? She couldn't imagine it. She just couldn't imagine it.

A week after she had moved into the Brand family home, dinnertime had become a comfortable routine. London and Barbara worked together in the kitchen while Hank tinkered in his study. Tyler always arranged to finish his work on the ranch so he could sit down at the dinner table with them. It wasn't what she had planned, but it had become an acceptable alternative.

"You're starting to show," Barbara noted as she turned over the chicken frying in the large black pan.

London's hands automatically went to her stomach. "I know. I could barely get these pants buttoned this morning."

"We'll have to take you shopping," Tyler's mom said. "Have the mints been helping?"

Barbara had bought her a bag of mints to help with the all-day sickness. London always had a handful of the red-and-white candies in her pocket.

"So far, so good."

Barbara turned the heat down before she helped London finish setting the table. "I remember how sick I was with Tyler. I had such an easy time with my first set of twins—Tyler's older brothers—that I wasn't really prepared to have a hard pregnancy.

"Then, with my second set of twins, the girls, I had another easy pregnancy. The only one who gave me a hard time was Tyler." Barbara laughed. "I gained a ton of weight and I was as sick as a dog. But it was worth it… Look what I got."

After dinner, Tyler and London insisted on washing the dishes while Barbara and Hank went for a walk. While the dinner routine had become more comfortable, the tension between Tyler and his father was palpable. She knew that the pregnancy was at the heart of this tension. Hank was a ring, marriage, *then* baby kind of man, and his middle child had defied that Brand family principle.

"I'm sorry things are still hard with your father." London put the last dish in the dishwasher and turned it on.

"He'll come around," Tyler assured her. "It's just going to take some time."

London had her back to Tyler, drying off her hands with a hand towel at the kitchen sink, when she felt him slip his arms around her waist and the warmth of his body on her back.

"I have a proposition for you," he whispered in her ear.

Her body went a little bonkers when Tyler was so close to her. Plain and simple, her body lusted for his body. She was in the stage of her pregnancy where she felt hungry, nauseous and horny *all the time*. She just wanted him to ravish her—no foreplay, no frills, just give it to her hard and nail her to the wall until this ache between her legs *stopped*.

She hadn't let herself go there with him. Sex had already complicated their lives enough. But how much frustration could one woman take? Tyler…sexy, strong, cowboy handsome Tyler was there for the taking. All she had to do was ask.

London slipped out from beneath his arms. She needed to put a safe distance between her body and the object of her desire.

"Which is?"

"Skinny-dipping. You and me. It's a full moon." Tyler put his arms around her waist again, nuzzled her neck. "Meet me on the porch at midnight?"

*Oh, heck with it.*

"Okay…"

They both knew where a midnight skinny-dip would lead. They both knew what she was ultimately saying yes to. Which was why there was a twinkle of anticipation in Tyler's clear blue eyes when he left the kitchen. And she had to be honest with herself—she couldn't wait for midnight.

That night, she lay flat on her back on top of the covers, fully clothed, waiting, waiting, waiting for midnight to arrive. When she heard the grandfather clock in the hallway begin to chime, she quickly slipped out of bed, down the two flights of stairs and out to the porch. Tyler was already waiting for her.

Laughing as quietly as she could manage, she took Tyler's outstretched hand and they both started to run away from the house. She felt like a teenager again, sneaking out of her parents' house to meet her first boyfriend. It was exhilarating.

The giant full moon cast a soft gold light that lit their way to the small lake behind Tyler's cabin. He had built the cabin on that plot of land specifically for the lake. He could walk out his back door, onto the short dock and jump in the lake to cool off during the summer.

Once they reached the dock, they were both winded and laughing.

"Why are we sneaking around like kids?" she asked him.

"Because my parents have hijacked this pregnancy. That's why!"

Tyler didn't waste any time disrobing. One minute he was dressed and the next minute he was naked in the moonlight. The man was an Adonis. That tall, lean body with long muscles that appeared to be sculpted from clay by a master's hands. She couldn't imagine that any woman would ever get tired of looking at Tyler Brand.

Tyler dived into the lake, leaving her standing on the dock. He shot upward out of the water, the water gleaming on his bare chest, and pushed his hair off his face.

"Come on, London," Tyler called to her. "The water's warm."

"Turn around."

"You're joking. I went with you to the ob-gyn!"

"I don't care," she whispered loudly. "Turn around."

"Fine." Tyler turned his back to her.

London quickly disrobed, padded over to the end of the dock and then dived headfirst into the water. Tyler turned around in time to see London, her athletic body naked and glowing in the light of the moon, execute a perfect dive into the middle of the lake. She was a goddess. Tyler swam toward her with every intention of making love to her as soon as he reached her.

## Chapter Eight

London emerged from the water and saw Tyler swimming toward her. She treaded water until he arrived at her side. She didn't resist when he took her in his arms and kissed the water from her lips. She took his tongue deep inside her mouth, silently giving her consent to him. He wanted to make love to her. She wanted to make love to him. This tension had been building between them for weeks. It wasn't a matter of *if*…it was always a matter of *when*.

Silently, they both swam to the embankment that had been cleared for sunbathing. Half in the water, half out, Tyler slipped between her legs and slipped his shaft into her body. Slow and hard, slow and hard, Tyler took command of her. She dropped her head back, eyes closed, overwhelmed by the sensations of pleasure Tyler was creating with his hands and his mouth and the thick shaft that filled her so completely.

Tyler loved his goddess with his entire body until he felt the sweet sensation of her orgasm. She didn't make a sound, but she dug her fingernails into his back and pushed against him with her hips. She was coming all around him, pulsing and writhing, inviting him to join her. Tyler sank deep within her body, head down, and groaned. The cool water swirled around their naked bodies while they caught their breath.

"Tyler...?"

"Hmm?"

"I don't want to ruin this otherwise superromantic moment...but I have mud in places where there shouldn't be mud..."

Tyler opened his eyes and looked down at her. "I can honestly say that I've never heard that one before."

They grabbed their clothing from the dock and ran, naked, into the cabin. Straight to the shower, they rinsed off under the warm water together and then got into Tyler's bed.

"It seems that you have returned to the scene of the crime." He propped himself up on his side to look at her.

"So it seems." She twisted her wet hair into a knot on top of her head.

"Regrets?"

"About tonight?" She sank back into the pillows. "I don't think so."

He glanced up at her with an odd look on his face. "No need to boost my ego."

She smiled at him. "You know what I mean."

"I'm teasing..." He threaded his fingers with hers

and kissed the back of her hand. "Tell me about your son."

It was an unexpected shift in conversation. "Now who's not being romantic?"

"I'm serious." He adjusted his body so he was sitting next to her, his back against the headboard. "Tell me about him."

"Do you want the long version or the short version?"

"I want whatever version you're willing to tell me," Tyler said seriously. "We have all night."

"I call him my love child." She glanced at him. "His father was my high school sweetheart…"

"First love?"

She nodded. "First everything. We both earned full-ride scholarships for basketball to the same university. My dad was so proud of me…" Her voice trailed off as if she were drifting away to another place. "But…then I got pregnant during my freshman year, lost my scholarship…and I gained my son."

"What about J.T.'s father?"

"Jon offered to give up his scholarship, but I wouldn't let him." She shrugged her shoulders. "He was so good. He had a real shot at the pros… I couldn't see any reason for both of us to give up our dreams.

"We stayed together for three years after J.T. was born. When he didn't get drafted by the NBA, he went to Canada to play ball, and…I don't know…after a while, we just didn't make sense anymore. Jon's a good father to J.T. and we're…cordial whenever we have to deal with each other. That's about it."

Tyler put his arms around her, hugged her and kissed her on the head affectionately. "Thank you."

"For what?"

"For sharing that with me." Tyler kept his arm around her and closed his eyes. "How old is J.T.?"

"Almost thirteen." London's eyes drooped closed. It was comfortable here in Tyler's arms. His body was solid and warm; he was a man a woman could learn to lean on.

"I have to get up," she murmured.

"Negative."

London forced herself to open her eyes and slide out of Tyler's embrace. She rolled out of bed so she could start getting dressed. She wasn't about to get caught doing a walk of shame from Tyler's cabin to the main house. Hank was an old-fashioned man who did not approve of her situation with his son. And for some reason, she wanted him to approve of her. Daddy issues, apparently.

"I'm keeping the T-shirt, FYI." London zipped her jeans. "Hey…are you going to walk me back, or what?"

Tyler hadn't moved. He was watching her through heavily lidded eyes. "I vote that you stay."

She pushed on his leg. "Come on. Get up."

With a disgruntled sigh, Tyler got up and got dressed.

"I think that you should move into my place tomorrow. We're adults. We shouldn't be sneaking around in the middle of the night like we're breaking curfew."

London had no intention of moving in with Tyler when his parents disapproved. They were the grandparents of her unborn child and their opinion mattered.

"Good night," London whispered.

Tyler caught her hand and stopped her from stepping up to the next step.

"Hey…tell me that you love me."

In the moonlight, Tyler could see the perplexed expression on her pretty face.

"Why would I say that to you?"

"Because it's true."

"Good night, Tyler…"

More loudly, he repeated himself. "Tell me that you love me, London."

"Shh…"

"Tell me…"

"*Fine*… I love you." She reclaimed her hand. "Good night."

The same day she officially withdrew from the fall semester was the same day she told her son that she was coming home for a visit. The happiness she heard in J.T.'s voice when she told him was a gift. And she couldn't wait to see him. To hug him. If only there wasn't a black cloud hanging over the entire trip.

"What about your classes?" J.T. asked her. He was such a smart kid.

"Let me worry about that," she hedged.

"I'll get Gram to pick us up one of those apartment guides from the grocery store."

London laughed. "I'm not going to be home long enough for that, J.T."

"I'll still ask her to get one just in case."

All J.T. had wanted for years was for them to have a place of their own. He loved his Gram and Pop, but she couldn't blame him for wanting to get out of their basement. Truth be told, she had sold him on the idea of Montana with the promise of it leading to a better job and a two-bedroom apartment just for them.

"I want to hear more about you." London changed the subject. "How's school?"

Now that she had an official date to face her family, she felt more relaxed. It was too hard to live with a secret. She was scared and excited all at once. Good, bad or indifferent, she would be heading home soon.

One of the best things about *not* leaving Bent Tree Ranch to finish her last semester was spending time with Rising Sun. Even though she still had a milder case of all-day sickness, she had forced herself to eat through the nausea and stay active. Being out in the barn and working with the handsome new colt kept her mind occupied and made her feel happy when she was having a sad day like today.

"Hey…"

London jumped at the sound of Tyler's voice. She had been lost in thought and hadn't realized that she wasn't alone anymore.

"Hi." She resumed the task of untangling Rising Star's long, thick mane.

Tyler noticed that she was wearing his Johnny Cash T-shirt and it made him feel good. It made him think that she wanted to be close to him even when he wasn't around.

"Mom told me that you withdrew from the semester today."

"It needed to be done." She had been putting it off and putting it off until the very last minute. It was hard to let go of something she had been working toward for so long. "I can be out for two semesters without reapplying."

He watched her methodically combing Star's mane. "Are you almost done with your day?"

"I'm done. I'm just diddling around now."

Tyler opened the latch to the stall gate. "Then I think you'd better come with me."

She followed Tyler out of the barn and noticed that there was an old-fashioned horse carriage rigged up in the common yard. London was immediately drawn to it.

"Where in the world did this come from?" She ran her hands over one of the four wooden-spoke wheels.

"My father is always looking for ways to surprise Mom on their anniversary. One year, he had this ladies' phaeton restored for her."

The phaeton had a tufted red velvet bench seat built for two and a black buggy top to protect occupants from the elements.

"It's so beautiful." London smiled.

"Climb on up," Tyler told her. "I'm taking you for a ride."

London spun her head around to look at him. "This is for me?"

Tyler looked directly into her eyes. "It's hard to be sad in a phaeton."

She climbed into the bench seat and Tyler joined her. He picked up the reins, released the brake, clucked his tongue, and the buggy lurched forward. The minute she felt the buggy move, London laughed. Tyler smiled at her. She knew that getting her to laugh and smile was why he had planned this buggy ride in the first place. Tyler steered the horses onto the main road so they could avoid some of the potholes characteristic of the less traveled roads on the ranch.

London held on to the edge of the seat, the wind in

her face, smiling. The ride was bumpy, which wasn't the best for her sensitive bladder, but she didn't care. She was having a blast and her stupid, annoying bladder would just have to wait!

"Do you want to drive?" Tyler asked her.

"Yes!"

"Scoot closer to me and I'll show you how to hold the reins."

Tyler halted the horses, put London's hands on the reins and then released the brake again. From the moment the horses started to move and she could feel the leashed power of steering two horses at once, London was hooked. The idea that she was doing something that women one hundred years before her time had done to travel made her feel connected to something bigger than herself. When they reached the end of the main road, her face muscles felt a little sore from the smiling and laughing. Tyler took over the reins so he could turn the buggy around while London slumped back into the soft velvet with a wide grin on her face.

"Thank you." She put her hand on his arm.

Tyler had turned the horses around. He halted the horses and put on the brake. With the sun setting in the distance, Tyler kissed her. It was a sweet, tender kiss, full of promise.

"You're welcome." Tyler touched her face gently. "You'll come to me tonight."

Was it a question? Was it a statement? She wasn't sure. And she didn't care.

"Yes." She linked her arm with his, leaned into his body. "I will."

That night, like a naughty teenager, she sneaked out of the main house and headed straight for Tyler's cabin.

When she opened the door, she saw that Tyler was waiting for her in the living room. It was chilly enough at night, even in the summer, for him to build a fire. He had a blanket laid out in front of the fire, and her stomach started to fill with nervous anticipation at the thought of making love with Tyler again.

He greeted her with a kiss. Then he undressed her in front of that fire, as if he was unwrapping a Christmas present. Layer by layer, her clothing was removed until she was standing completely naked before him, bathed in firelight.

Tyler was mesmerized by London's beauty. The changes in her body from the pregnancy, camouflaged when she was clothed, were on display for his hungry eyes. Her breasts were larger now, rounder and fuller. Her waist, still long and thin, curved down to the noticeable bump. Tyler knelt down before her and splayed his hands over her belly.

"Lie down," he told her.

They lay down together on the blanket. She was on her back while Tyler was on his side facing her. He rested his hand on her baby bump.

"What can I do for you?"

It was a lover's question. He wanted to serve her, but was she brave enough to ask for what she really needed?

"My breasts are so sore," she admitted. "They hurt all the time now."

"What can I do?"

"Massage them."

He told her to close her eyes, relax and let him make her feel better. He filled his hands with her swollen, aching breasts and began to massage them. She moaned and turned her head toward the fire. His large hands were strong from years of ranch work. The harder he squeezed, the better she liked it. It was releasing the pain, releasing the ache.

When he heard her sigh happily and smile, he replaced his hands with his mouth. He kissed her neck and her breasts before he dropped several kisses on the baby bump on his way to his final destination. He nudged open her thighs with his hand so he could taste her. It felt so good, so right, that she cried out from the pleasure of it. He worshipped her with his mouth until she reached for him.

They made love in front of the fire. But it wasn't enough for London. The pregnancy hormones had made her crazy horny. She wanted it all the time. They moved to the bedroom and when Tyler was able, they made love again.

"Tell me what you want." Tyler was on top of her, inside her.

"I want it as hard as you can give it to me."

Tyler grabbed the headboard for leverage so he could give her exactly what she asked him for. He drove into her again and again until he felt her start to climax. London bit Tyler's shoulder to stop herself from screaming so loudly that they could hear her in the main house. When it was over, they looked at each other and started to laugh.

"That was…" Tyler rolled onto his back. "I don't know what that was…"

Naked, completely satiated, London shook her head in wonder and smiled a small smile. There weren't any words for what they had just experienced together. It had been so off-the-charts amazing it felt otherworldly.

They both closed their eyes to catch their breath. In

the quiet, now that she was still, she noticed something strange happening. Tiny little contractions. Alarmed, London sat up and put her hand on her baby bump.

"What's wrong?" Tyler propped himself up on his elbow.

"I don't know… I feel something…like little contractions near my cervix."

Tyler sat up completely, his eyes focused on her stomach. "Were we too rough?"

"Maybe. I don't know," she said, her hand still on her stomach. "I didn't have sex the last time I was pregnant."

"What should we do?" Tyler's voice was tight and tense.

"I don't know." London felt a swell of tears start to form.

"Here…just lie down." Tyler stacked the pillows behind her. "If they don't subside, we'll go to the hospital."

London lay back on the pillows and Tyler covered her with the blanket. She closed her eyes and started to pray that the baby would be okay. She had been so angry that she was pregnant. She had been so frustrated that she had to change her plans because of the baby that she had detached herself from the life growing within her. Until now. Until this moment. She wanted this baby. No matter what changes she had to make, no matter how challenging, for the first time since she'd discovered that she was pregnant, she genuinely *wanted* Tyler's child.

They sat together, Tyler by her side, for a tense fifteen minutes until the sensation stopped. London closed her eyes gratefully and thanked God. Her prayers were answered. She felt more connected to her baby. She felt more connected to Tyler.

"I wouldn't do anything to hurt you or our baby," Tyler said apologetically.

"It's not your fault, Tyler," she assured him. "I think we were just a little too rough. That's all. I feel better now."

"I think we need to stop fooling around until we see the doctor next week."

"Let's not overreact…"

"Nope." Tyler shook his head emphatically. "I'm sorry, but I'm cutting you off."

Tyler was as good as his word. She was discovering that about him. No matter how she tried to entice him, he refused to make love to her until the doctor gave them the green light. They received positive news about the pregnancy during her routine appointment—her weight was on target, her morning sickness was under control and they were given the green light to have *gentle* intercourse. After the doctor, they went next door for another ultrasound.

"And here's your baby…" The technician moved the wand across London's abdomen.

Tyler leaned forward, his eyes fixed on the monitor. This ultrasound image was so much different than the last. The image of the baby on the screen…*his baby*…stunned him. The last time they had an ultrasound, the baby had been just a small black dot with a heartbeat. Now, it looked like a real baby.

"There's the face and the eyes and the nose…" The technician pointed out the features as they became visible. "We've caught the baby sucking its thumb."

"Can you tell yet?" London asked.

"Not yet…" The technician knew she was referring

to gender. "The legs are in the wrong position. Next time."

After the appointment, they went shopping for jeans that could see London through the next couple months. They stopped by the baby section, and then at Tyler's insistence, they stopped by the jewelry counter.

"What do you like?" Tyler asked her. "I never see you wearing jewelry."

"I don't really." She studied the ring options in the case. "I have always liked emeralds."

"Yellow or white gold?"

"Yellow."

They were talking around the issue, but they both knew that they were discussing an engagement ring. Tyler had made it clear from the very beginning that he wanted to marry her and raise their child at Bent Tree Ranch. She had grown to love the land as much as he did. But it wasn't just about her or Tyler or even the baby on the way. She had a son in Virginia who was waiting for her to come home.

"Penny for your thoughts," Tyler said to her on the drive home.

"I was just thinking that the baby looks like you."

"You think so?"

She nodded.

"I tell you what…" Tyler gave a little shake of his head. "I don't know our child yet, I don't know if it's a boy or a girl…and I want you to know that I don't care either way. I don't even know our child's name, but when I saw him, or her, on the screen today…" He shook his head in wonder again. "The love I felt for that baby… I didn't even know I had that much love in my heart."

## Chapter Nine

She had been living a double life and it was starting to weigh heavily on her. Her family in Virginia didn't know that she had withdrawn from school or that she was pregnant and still living at the ranch. It was easy to blur the truth when you were hundreds of miles away.

And she had been lying to Tyler, really. Lying by omission. He believed that they were slowly building a life together in Montana. Part of her wanted to believe that was possible, too. But nothing was certain. Nothing. If she had to choose between being with her son or staying in Montana with Tyler, she would choose her son every single time.

"I wasn't expecting to find you here." Tyler walked through the chapel door carrying a toolbox.

London hadn't expected anyone to be up at the chapel this time of day. For weeks now, it had been a place of retreat, a place of quiet reflection for her.

She stood up to face him. "I like to come up here to think."

"Well...don't let me stop you." Tyler put the toolbox down on one of the benches. "I'm just dropping this off for later." Tyler nodded at her hands. "What's that?"

London walked over to him, hands open. "It's my grandmother's rosary. She was devout."

"It's beautiful." Tyler added with a facetious smile, "Are things so bad that you need to pray?"

When she didn't laugh, he asked the question again, but this time without the joking smile. "Are things so bad that you need to pray about them?"

"Do you have time to sit down with me?" she asked.

"I'll make the time."

They sat down on the bench closest to the preacher's podium. London reached for Tyler's hand. This man had been so honest with her, so true. From the very beginning, he had never wavered in his desire to make a family with her. All of his cards were on the table. She was the one with secrets. She was the one who was always hiding something.

"I want you to know that...I think that I've loved you from the first day we met. But I couldn't allow myself to get involved. I had J.T. to think about and I couldn't let myself get sidetracked *again* because of a man...do you understand that?"

"Why does this sound like you're trying to say goodbye to me?"

"I just want you to understand why I've always... put walls up between us." She looked down at their entwined fingers. "Things with my son are complicated,

Tyler. His father has joint custody, but he's wanted J.T. to live with him for a while now. And the only reason J.T. is in Virginia with my parents is because both sets of grandparents are there and J.T. didn't want to leave his friends."

"J.T.'s father wouldn't agree to him moving to Montana, is that what you're worried about?"

"I think there is zero chance that Jon will agree to it. He'll fight me for full custody and I'm not altogether sure that he wouldn't win. I can't risk losing my son, Tyler. I can't do it."

"Hey…don't get yourself all worked up over something that hasn't happened yet. You don't know that he'd win full custody…"

Tears started to spill onto her cheeks—tears that she had been holding back for months. Tyler wiped her tears away with his thumbs and then pulled her into his arms.

"If I stay in Montana with you…" She pushed back a little to she could look into his eyes. "And I do want to stay in Montana with you, Tyler, I do…but I think that he'd have a very good case against me."

"Why's that?"

London wiped her face off on her shirt and pulled her phone out of her back pocket. "You've never asked to see a picture of my son."

"I didn't want to push you…"

She held out her phone to him. "That's J.T."

Tyler looked at the picture of the boy. He was a tall kid, stocky, with a round face and a quirky grin.

"Good-looking kid," Tyler observed.

"That's it?"

"What did you expect me to say?"

"Did you notice that he's biracial? His father is African-American."

"I can see pretty good." Tyler handed the phone back to her. "I just didn't think it needed to be mentioned."

"Well…his father thinks it's worth mentioning. Jon thinks it's of utmost importance for J.T. to be connected to his culture. And he doesn't think that I'm equipped to do that." London gestured around her. "If Jon gets wind of the fact that I'm trying to move his son to a state that has—let's face it—not much diversity… I think the gloves will come off."

Tyler took a minute or two to process all of the information London had shared. Finally, he took both of her hands in his and said, "Look…if we're in for a fight, we're in for a fight. But let's not borrow trouble. We'll just take it one step at a time. You'll be seeing J.T. at the end of the month, and you can get him used to the idea of the baby and coming to Montana for a visit," Tyler said. "Why don't we fly him out here the next time he has a break for school? Once he's here, I guarantee he'll fall in love with the place. After all, some of the first cowboys were black. It's in his DNA to love it here."

London nodded her agreement. "His father has him for Thanksgiving, but I get him for Christmas this year."

"Then we'll bring him here for Christmas at Bent Tree Ranch." Tyler squeezed her hands to reassure her. "Until then…let's just take things one day at a time. We're here together now." He kissed her lightly on the lips. "That's all that matters to me."

London put her hands on either side of his face. "I love you, Tyler."

Tyler gazed into the eyes of the woman he loved,

the mother of his first child. "And I love you. From the first moment I saw your face, I've had you in my heart."

That night, London went to bed with less weight on her shoulders. She had opened her heart to Tyler and he had treated it gently. She still had her reservations about J.T.'s ability to thrive in Montana, much less his father's agreement to such a move. But she had Tyler in her corner. This time, this pregnancy, she wasn't alone.

"London! London!" Banging on the wall at the bottom of the stairs awakened her. In the dark, she fumbled for the light by the side of the bed.

"London! London!" More banging on the wall—it was Barbara calling her name.

She shoved the blanket back, swung her legs out of bed and ran to the door. She ran down three flights of stairs and down the hallway to the back of the house. She had never been to this part of the farmhouse—this was where the master bedroom was located. In her bare feet, she walked quickly to the end of the hall.

"Damn it, Barb… I'm fine." Hank was sitting on the edge of the bed; his typically tanned face was ashen. He appeared to be out of breath and had broken out into a sweat.

"What's wrong?"

"Nothing!" Hank snapped at his wife. "It's a stomach bug, nothing more. Go back upstairs."

"You hush up!" Barbara snapped back at Hank. "He woke up with stomach pains and pains in his arm and his back."

London stayed in the doorway. "Any shortness of breath?"

Grudgingly, Hank said, "A little."

"Chest pains?" It was like reliving her stepfather's heart attack all over again.

"They...they come and go," Hank admitted.

"Aspirin?" London asked Barb.

"I'll get it." Barbara headed to the bathroom and returned quickly with water and an aspirin.

"I'll call an ambulance," London said. Hank had all the symptoms of a heart attack.

"No." Barb shook her head. "Go wake Tyler...the ambulance will take forever. We'll drive him in ourselves."

London could hear Hank protesting as she ran through the house, out the front door and across the yard to the cabin. Tyler was easy to wake, and then the four of them piled in to Hank's king-cab truck and headed to Helena. They arrived at the emergency room and Hank was immediately taken back on priority. It wasn't a surprise to London when the tests confirmed that Hank had a blockage in one of his arteries.

"What's the word?" Tyler stood up when his mom appeared in the waiting room.

"They're admitting him," his mother said. "They've given him some medicine to dissolve the blockage, but we'll just have to wait and see. They're calling in the specialist tomorrow. You two go on back to the ranch—I'm going to stay here with your father."

"I don't want to leave you here, Mom."

"No. Really, Tyler...please go back to the ranch. It causes me more stress worrying about the two of you on top of worrying about your dad. London looks exhausted—she needs her rest."

"I'm okay," London protested.

Barbara had the last word. She was the matriarch of the family. She hugged and kissed both of them, and then sent them on their way with a wave and a promise to call with an update. She tasked Tyler with calling all of his siblings in the morning, along with any relevant family members and friends.

When they arrived back at the ranch, the sun was still several hours from coming up. They first went to the main house to get Ilsa, the German shepherd, and Ranger, the cat, before they headed to the cabin. They undressed, slipped into bed together and Tyler wrapped his arm around London, his hand possessively resting on her baby bump. Ilsa spread out at the bottom of the bed, while Ranger took possession of the spot above their heads. For several hours they slept together, until the light of the sun filtered through the open window. Tyler rolled over and squinted at the sun streaming in the window before he carefully extracted his arm from beneath London's head. Ilsa and Ranger were both waiting at the door to be let out. He took care of the animals first before he took care of himself.

"How's Dad?" Tyler had his cell phone on speaker while he started the coffee.

"Ticked," his mother said with a yawn. "He thinks this is all just a big waste of time. Have you called your brother and your sisters?"

"Doing that next. How are you holding up?"

"I'm fine, honey. I'll call you later."

Tyler called his siblings and then searched in his kitchen for breakfast food options that wouldn't irritate London's overly sensitive sense of smell. After a breakfast of plain toast with peanut butter, which London managed to keep down, they hung out near the main house until they heard from Barb.

* * *

Hank was released from the hospital two days later with a confirmed diagnosis of a mild heart attack. Anyone who knew Hank realized that it would be an uphill battle getting him to agree to the recommended heart-healthy diet, which was the topic of discussion the morning after his release from the hospital.

Hank looked at the small plate his wife had put down in front of him with a mixture of confusion, irritation and disgust.

"What happened to the rest of my breakfast?" he asked Barb.

She joined them at the table with her own small plate. "This is it. Scrambled eggs, wheat toast and a sliced banana."

To London she said, "I have to go into town today and stock up on some things—do you want to come with me?"

"Barb..." Hank used a tone of voice that London had never heard him use before with his wife. "I'm not going to be changing every little thing just because I had a few chest pains."

Hank loved bacon and butter and steak and sausage and everything else that had appeared in the *avoid* column of the heart-healthy diet list. Tyler and London exchanged glances and decided to keep their opinions to themselves.

"I do the cooking and this is what I made," Barbara said easily. "If you want something else, you'll have to make it yourself."

Hank put the plate on the floor for Ilsa, stood up more slowly than he usually would, went to his study and shut the door behind him hard.

Barbara continued to eat her scrambled eggs. "Change is always difficult."

"I remember how tough it was for my stepdad to change his lifestyle after his heart attack," London agreed.

They all felt as though they had dodged a bullet with this heart attack—it was a warning. Hank had heart disease and if he didn't change his diet, he would end up on the operating table—or worse. But everyone in the family knew that he was going to be stubborn about it. He was a rancher. He liked to eat red meat and smoke cigars.

"Once he comes to terms with it, it'll be easier. He's going to be a bear as long as he's on light duty," Barbara said thoughtfully. "For now, we're all just going to have to support him with a lot of love and patience. Nobody likes to get this kind of news."

Tyler went to work and London went into town with Barb, armed with a list of healthier foods for the refrigerator. While they were buying groceries, it occurred to London that she should do something to spoil Tyler. He had been completely supportive from the first moment they discovered that she was pregnant. He'd never wavered in his commitment to her or their child. She knew that she hadn't been able, for a multitude of reasons, to commit to him with the same confidence. Tyler had been doing most of the heavy lifting in their unconventional relationship, and she wanted to let him know that she recognized it and appreciated it.

While Tyler was moving the herd to a different pasture, she took over his kitchen and started to make his favorite meal: shepherd's pie. Barb's recipe was simple enough to follow. So, the minute they got back to the ranch, she started peeling potatoes to mash. With the potatoes in the pot boiling on the stove, London tied a bandanna over her face, like a train robber from an old Western movie, so she could brown the hamburger meat without smelling it. She browned the meat as quick as possible, breathing through her mouth, then added cans of strained corn to the browned hamburger.

After she browned the meat, she had to go outside for some fresh air. For her, it was definitely challenging to cook while pregnant. Back in the kitchen, London mashed the potatoes using salted butter and heavy whipping cream. She dug through the bottom kitchen cabinets to find a glass pan that would be perfect for baking, spread the meat mixture on the bottom, added a layer of mashed potatoes and then topped off the pie with freshly grated sharp cheddar cheese. Finally, she popped the shepherd's pie into the oven to bake.

She sat in Tyler's living room, trying not to think about all of the things that she was missing this semester in school and back in Virginia with her son as he started middle school. This was an important milestone and she was missing it. She had thought, at the time, that the events she missed would be counterbalanced by the security a degree would bring. But now? What was that payoff? What had she done to herself? What had she done to her son?

"Man...something smells good in here!" Tyler opened the front door of the cabin.

London quickly wiped the tears from her eyes and pasted a welcoming smile on her face. She met him halfway for a hug. He kissed her hello on the lips before he leaned down to kiss her baby bump.

With his arm still around her, holding her close to him, he said, "I could get used to this."

"Please don't." She laughed, happy to see him. "I need to be out in the barn. I love your mom and dad, but their arrangement would drive me insane."

"So...I can't ask you to fetch me a beer and my slippers?"

She hugged him with another laugh. "Not if you want to keep your front teeth."

"I want to keep them," he assured her.

She took his hand and led him into the kitchen. When she opened the oven to show Tyler what was baking, his eyes lit up.

"I thought I smelled Mom's shepherd's pie!" Tyler eyed the pan hungrily.

London opened the refrigerator and waved her arm as if she was a hostess on a game show. "And...your favorite beer."

Her plan to spoil him had worked. Tyler leaned back against the kitchen counter with a look of sheer pleasure and surprise on his good-looking face.

"What's the occasion?" he asked her.

London didn't often feel embarrassment, nor was she a shy person. But the way Tyler was looking at her, with his deeply set clear blue eyes filled with such love and admiration, made her feel more shy and self-conscious than she had in her life.

Her face felt a little hot. Was she actually blushing? "I just wanted to do something nice for you, that's all. Why don't you go get cleaned up? By the time you're done with your shower, dinner will be ready."

They ate dinner on the back deck of the cabin, with the small lake and dock in the foreground, and the cha-

pel on the hill and the tall mountains as the background.
It was more romantic than any fancy restaurant could
have been. It seemed as if they were the only two people on the planet. Tyler had three helpings of the shepherd's pie, which made her feel like a million bucks,
because Barbara Brand was a hard act to follow in the
kitchen. He wouldn't let her clear the table or wash the
dishes. Instead, he piled them up in the sink, bachelor-
style. They sat down at the end of the dock, him with his
last beer in hand and her with her toes dangling in the
lake water that was cooling with the early-evening air.

"This is the life," Tyler said, looking out at the ranch
he loved.

She nodded, swirling circles in the water with her
toes. Life on a Montana ranch was a distant dream that
she'd thought could never happen. Unlike Tyler, she still
wasn't entirely certain that it could.

"You know what I was thinking?" Tyler put down
his half-empty bottle of beer. "We could build an ex-
tension on the cabin so J.T. can have his own room. He
could design it any way he wanted."

"You already have him moved in..." She pulled her
feet out of the water and crossed her legs beneath her.
"How can you be so certain of everything?"

Tyler shrugged. "I see it, just as clearly as I see those
mountains...just as clearly as I see you."

She cocked her head to the side, leaned her chin on
her shoulder to look at him. There was no sense trying
to change his mind—he had already decided that his
vision of the future was an accurate one. But she had
nothing but doubts. J.T. was an urban kid. He played
on a basketball team at her mother's church and all he
talked about was making junior varsity at the middle

school. He loved to skateboard with his friends at the local skate park. He wore sneakers and baseball caps, not cowboy boots and cowboy hats. As hard as she tried, she couldn't see J.T. taking to ranch life. If J.T. didn't love it, there would be no convincing Jon.

"Could you ever imagine yourself anywhere else? Other than Bent Tree?" she asked him.

Tyler polished off his beer. "Never." He looked into the distance, like the king surveying his kingdom. "I feel like I'm a part of this land...like I was built from this dirt and these rocks and this clay... I'd never be happy anywhere else but here."

She had already known the answer to her question, but she had felt compelled to ask it anyway. If J.T. couldn't be happy, truly happy, on the ranch, then she couldn't stay. She had grown to love Tyler, his family and this ranch deeply...and she was acutely aware of the pain she would cause him if she separated him from his firstborn child. Their future happiness was pinned on her son's acceptance of this huge shift in lifestyle and she hadn't even told him that he would be traveling to Montana for Christmas.

"Are you up for a swim?" Tyler asked.

"After all of that shepherd's pie you ate? You'll sink!"

Tyler leaned toward her for a kiss. "I'll stay in the shallow end."

They swam together in the lake, made love in the shower, and Tyler brushed her long hair in front of the fire. Lying in his arms, her hand on his chest, her head resting on his shoulder, London couldn't remember a time when she'd felt this happy. This comfortable. Yes, there were so many things that were unsettled and uncertain, but this moment was perfect.

"I told your mom that you asked me to marry you..."

Tyler opened his eyes. "You did? Why?"

She burrowed her nose into his neck. "Because I wanted her to hear it from me that you had tried to do the right thing by me and this child."

"I love my parents. I respect them. But what matters to me is that *you* know I'm doing right by you and our child."

"You're not upset with me for telling her...?"

"No. Just don't want you to think that you have to fix anything. Me and my folks will always be fine. That's not for you to worry about."

"Okay." She breathed in the scent of his skin. Tyler always smelled so good to her.

Tyler turned his body so they were facing each other, his back to the fire.

"You know..." he murmured. "Pretty soon we're going to find out if we're having a boy or a girl."

"That's true..."

"Have you been thinking about names?"

"Some..." She didn't feel like talking now. "You?"

"I've thought about it."

When he didn't continue, she said, "Is it a secret?"

He dropped a kiss on her head with a laugh. "No. It's not a secret. If we have a boy in there, I'd like to name him after my grandfather... Conrad."

She thought about the name. It was a good strong name. "Conrad Brand."

"It's got a ring to it, right?"

"I like it. And for a girl?"

"Still keepin' it in the family," Tyler said. "Margaret... for my grandmother."

"Margaret Brand. It's a name she'll have to grow in

to. We could call her Maggie for short." London snuggled closer to Tyler. "Conrad or Maggie."

That night, London fell asleep in Tyler's arms without a thought about returning to her third-floor bedroom in the main house. She knew where she belonged now—she belonged in Tyler's house, in Tyler's bed, in Tyler's arms. And now that she knew, truly knew, she didn't want to spend even one more night away from him.

## *Chapter Ten*

While Barbara was occupied with Hank's recovery, London made a slow but steady transition from the main house to Tyler's cabin. She had rearranged some of the furniture in the living room and organized the odd collection of cooking items that Tyler kept in his kitchen. The more time she spent in the cabin, the more she began to imagine herself there, with her son, full-time. It wasn't the ideal place for a family—Tyler had built it to be a bachelor pad without much thought of a future wife or children. But he wasn't really attached to the cabin's interior or exterior. He was willing to change it to make it work for her, the baby and her son. The cabin, the ranch…Tyler…they were all starting to feel like home.

"Tyler Brand! Are you in here!"

A female voice at the front door startled London.

She threw the pillows on the bed and went into the living room. Sophia Brand, wife of Tyler's older brother, Luke, was standing just inside the front door.

"He's worming the herd in the south pasture with Clint and Brock today," London told Sophia. "He won't be back until later on."

"London!" Sophia smiled warmly. "Mom told us you were still here!"

Sophia was a hugger. She hugged London in greeting before she sat down on the couch.

Sophia looked around. "It looks different in here. Bigger."

Not sitting down, London shifted uncomfortably. How much did Sophia know about her relationship with Tyler?

"I didn't know that you were coming for a visit so soon," London said.

Sophia pulled her ponytail holder out, pulled her honey-blond hair back and then made a new ponytail. "Neither did we." She waved her hand. "Sit, sit…let's catch up."

London sat at the other end of the couch, but she didn't lean back or get comfortable. Sophia and Luke had been at the ranch for Jordan's wedding, but she had hardly spoken more than two words to either of them. She could tell by Sophia's demeanor—and from the things Tyler had said about her—that Tyler's sister-in-law considered everyone to be a friend. She had openness in her pretty hazel eyes and dimpled smile that were hallmarks of her sweet personality.

"Can we just talk about the elephant in the room?" Sophia looked at her directly in the eyes. "I know you and Tyler are pregnant."

Why she should be surprised, she didn't know. But she was. "Did Barb tell you?"

"Not directly, no." Sophia leaned back. "She's a vault when she wants to be. But wedding central is now baby central. You're making out like a bandit."

London had had no idea that Barb was stockpiling baby items in the main house.

"I didn't know that…"

Sophia tucked one leg under the other with a smile. "Well…don't be mad at her. Mom loves to spoil grand-children."

"I'm not mad…just surprised," she said. "Are your children with you?"

Sophia's eyes brightened at the mention of her children. "Yes. The gang's all here! Luke wanted to come home when he heard about Hank's health problems, so we decided to just make a family trip of it… That's what I love about Bent Tree…open-door policy."

They chatted for a little while longer before Sophia said that she had to get back to the main house to check on the kids.

"Four and two," Sophia said of her older son and her twin girls. "They're a handful."

Sophia walked to the front door with a jaunty step. "You guys are coming to the main house for dinner, aren't you?"

"Yes. I always help Barb with dinner."

"Perfect!" Sophia smiled at her with a genuine smile. "And London, congratulations on the baby. Welcome to the family."

That night, dinner at the main house was a raucous affair. With six additional people around the table, the kitchen was filled with loud voices and laughter and the sounds of toddlers trying to get attention. London loved the way Tyler's family interacted with one another. They teased each other, but it was always in good humor and good fun. Her family was smaller and much more reserved. Dinnertime was often quiet. Not so with the Brands.

"You know…" Sophia wiped one of her daughters' faces. "It's hard to believe that I was pregnant with Danny here at the ranch during Christmastime…and now look at him, sitting at the table like a big boy."

London was sitting across from Sophia and Luke's son. She asked him, "How old are you, Danny?"

Danny, a towheaded boy with Sophia's dimples and Luke's bright blue eyes, held up four fingers while he continued to chew.

London looked at the twin girls sitting in high chairs next to the table. She'd always wanted a girl and hoped in her heart that the child she was carrying turned out to be a Maggie. "Your girls are beautiful—but I really can't tell them apart."

"This little munchkin—" Sophia kissed her daughter's cheek "—is Abigail, my deep thinker. And this sweet little thing—" she touched the head of her other daughter "—is Annabelle…my daredevil. I can't believe that they just turned two. Time is flying."

Luke, a retired marine, turned to Hank, who had resumed his place at the head of the table. "Bonfire tonight?"

"That's exactly what I was thinking, son." Hank stacked his utensils on his empty plate. "Tonight's a special occasion. I'm going to smoke my last cigar."

The table was cleared, the dishes were washed and the twins were put down for the night. For the first time that London could remember, Barbara joined them at the bonfire. Tyler's mom had always given Hank his opportunity to sneak a cigar, but tonight was different.

Tyler had grabbed his guitar and Sophia had grabbed a bag of jumbo marshmallows. Tonight would be Danny's first time toasting marshmallows at the bonfire.

"It's too bad your aunt Josephine isn't here now… she's the one who really knows how to toast a marshmallow to perfection." Sophia helped her son hold a long carved toasting stick near the flames of the fire.

London looked around the bonfire. Barbara and Hank were sitting close together on a log, their shoulders and their legs touching, smiling at each other as if they were newlyweds. Tyler was tuning his guitar while Sophia blew on her son's flaming marshmallow. Luke, the eldest of Hank and Barb's brood, was nearby chopping wood so he could make the bonfire burn hotter and brighter. She could imagine her son enjoying a night like this, surrounded by people who loved each other through their problems. If J.T. could embrace the ranch, London believed that they could have a good, decent, loving life at Bent Tree.

"This…" Hank pulled a fresh cigar from the pocket of his faded butter-yellow chambray and held it up for everyone to see. "Is my last cigar."

Hank waved it in front of his nose, closed his eyes and sniffed it lovingly. London had been at the ranch long enough to know how much Hank Brand loved his cigars. Hank opened his eyes and looked at the cigar for a few seconds before he tossed it into the bonfire.

Hank looked down at his bride of nearly fifty years.

"I promise you that I'm done with 'em, starting right now."

Barbara kissed her husband and hugged him tight.

"I'm proud of you, Dad." Luke returned to the fire. He tossed the extra logs on the bonfire before he sat down.

Luke was a man of very few words. Tyler had told her that a career in the marines and several tours to Afghanistan had changed his older brother. London wondered how Sophia, who was personable and bubbly, had ended up with such a quiet, introspective man.

"I meant to tell you…what happened the other night—" London noticed that Hank never actually used the words *heart attack* "—really spooked my mule."

Barbara smiled up at her husband. "Well—I'm *glad* it spooked your mule. It needed to be spooked."

Tyler started to play a Willie Nelson tune on his guitar while Danny loaded three marshmallows on his stick to put in the fire.

"While we're all together, I may as well let you guys in on the deal." Luke poked the fire with a large stick. He wasn't looking at anyone in particular when he said, "Sophia and I are moving the family to Montana."

Tyler stopped playing. Sophia used her free hand to reach out and touch her husband. Luke took Sophia's offered hand when he looked at his parents.

"What about your work at the crisis hotline? What about Sophia's practice?" Barbara asked. "Not that I want to talk you out of it… I'd rather have all of my children back in Montana."

"We haven't really worked out the details…" Sophia smiled, but London detected a world of worries behind that sweet, reassuring smile.

"Well…you know that there's always been a piece of Brand land with your name on it, Luke…and little Danny there inherited Daniel's piece…so you've got a pretty nice chunk of land to build a home and run a herd if you want."

Luke shook his head. "I'm no rancher, Dad… I'll leave that to you and Tyler." Luke turned to his wife. "Sophia and I'll have to talk about the land."

Sophia's laugh was tinny and uncertain. "We have a lot to talk about. A lot to work out…"

Next to Sophia, crying from one of the twins came over the baby monitor. "That's my cue." To her husband she said, "I'll see you and Danny back at the house."

Sophia kissed her husband and son before she excused herself and went back. London curled her knees up to her chest, pulled her sleeves down over her hands and looked up at the moon, so round and full and glowing in the large expanse of the Montana night sky. Along with Hank and Barbara, she was listening to Tyler play the guitar while the bonfire crackled and popped and sent tiny orange pieces of ash into the air. She had not intended to be here, with the Brand family, at this time of year. She had thought to be immersed in her last semester by now. But did she regret it? Right now, tonight…could she say that she was sorry this pregnancy had changed her path and forever linked her destiny with the destiny of the Brand family? No. She couldn't regret it. Not anymore.

Several hours slipped by and one by one, the family dispersed. Little Danny, his face and hands sticky with melted marshmallow, was shepherded back to the main house by Luke; Hank and Barbara turned in soon after.

"I love your family," she told Tyler.

Tyler had put down his guitar and was kicking some dirt onto the flames.

"Yeah…I lucked out, I'd say." He patted the spot next to him. "Why are you so far away from me?"

She laughed. Tyler was the first man she'd been involved with who was never shy about the fact that he liked to be near her. She scooted over closer to him and when she was within reach, Tyler put his arm around her and pulled her into his body.

"Now, this is what I like," Tyler said.

"Hmm." He had a point. This *was* nice.

"I don't know what to make of Luke moving back to Montana. But I'm sure I'll get the full story when Luke's ready to tell it."

"He's so…quiet," London said.

"I guess with all of us motormouths, there had to be one quiet one." Tyler laughed. "He's always been quiet, but the military changed him. He wasn't so serious all of the time. He wasn't so…"

"Watchful?"

"Yeah…that's a good word for it. It's like he's always on alert, like he's expecting a fight to break out or a bomb to go off," Tyler said. "If it weren't for Sophia and the kids, I don't know how adjusted Luke would be."

"Sophia's a sweetheart."

Tyler turned his head so he could breathe in the honeysuckle scent of London's freshly washed hair. "That she is."

They sat together, leaning on each other, until the fire died down and the chill of the night air was too cool for their lightweight clothing. It had become a silent agreement between Tyler's parents and them…she was with him in the cabin at night. She started to wonder how she had ever slept alone.

They started out in the spooning position, with Tyler's long limbs wrapped possessively around her body, until it got too hot. Then they both slept side by side, feet and hands touching, on their backs. It was the perfect arrangement. Some nights, Tyler would wake her up in the most sensual of ways…his mouth on her breast, his hand gently coaxing her thighs apart. And some nights she was the one to wake him up with a lover's kiss. She could vividly remember how it felt to be pregnant with J.T., alone and sexually frustrated to the max. With this pregnancy, whenever she wanted it…whenever she flat-out *needed* it, Tyler was there. He was always there.

"Damn it, Ell! When'd you move the chair?" Tyler cursed in the early-morning light.

London burrowed deeper into the bed and smiled sheepishly. "Sorry! Nesting!"

Today was a special day—they were going in to Helena to find out the sex of the baby. Tyler had awakened, as usual, before dawn and intended to work on one of the tractors that had been on the blink. She intended to spend some time with Rising Sun, gentling him to a blanket on his back. Besides spending time with Tyler, spending time with the black colt was her happy space. She could lose herself for a whole afternoon with the future champion.

"How's the nausea?" Tyler handed her chamomile tea with a little honey.

London sat upright to take the cup. She blew on the hot drink. "Not bad. Better lately."

The horrible all-day sickness during the first trimester and half of the second trimester had slowly begun to subside. It felt as though she was finally settling in to the pregnancy.

Tyler sat down on the bed next to her and put on his socks before he grabbed a bunched-up T-shirt out of a drawer and pulled it over his head.

"What's on your agenda?" Tyler stretched his arms above his head.

"Rising Sun."

Tyler leaned over to give her a quick kiss. "Why am I not surprised? I'm going to grab some coffee up at the main house. Want me to wait for you?"

"Uh-uh...you get going. I'll meet you back here at ten thirty?"

Tyler headed out the door. "Ow! Damn it, Ell!"

"Watch out for the chair!" she teased him.

She took her time getting out of bed, enjoyed her tea and then got dressed for barn work. She planned on getting back to the cabin in time to take a shower for her doctor's appointment. She spent several hours in the barn, working with the colt. She returned to the cabin to get ready for the trip to Helena. Once she was out of the shower and dressed, she couldn't seem to sit still. She washed the dishes that Tyler had left in the sink, cleaned out some of the old leftovers and contemplated a different furniture arrangement for the living room. She obsessively checked the clock on the stove—Tyler could get lost in his work. Today of all days, she wanted to be on time. As it turned out, Tyler must have felt the same way, because he returned to the cabin early, jumped in the shower and was ready to go by ten. It was smooth sailing all the way to Helena, and they didn't have to wait long to see the doctor or to get called back for the ultrasound. It felt as if they were completely in the flow.

"Okay…" London smoothed her hands over her stomach. "Last chance…what's your gut tellin' you—girl or boy?"

Tyler put down the fishing magazine he'd brought with him from the waiting room. "Boy. One hundred percent."

London inspected the white ceiling tiles above her head. "I think it's a Maggie. That's what I think."

She had taken to thinking of their baby as Maggie. In her mind, she called the baby Maggie. Was that wishful thinking or a mother's instinct? She would find out sooner than later.

Joy, who had been their technician for every ultrasound appointment, entered the room with a greeting and a smile.

"Are you ready to find out the sex of the baby today?"

"More than ready." London held out her hand to Tyler. "Right?"

Tyler took her hand. "I'm ready."

Joy put the gel on London's abdomen. "This'll be a little warm."

With the wand, the technician began the ultrasound. "Here's a face looking at you…and we have a really good view today of the baby's legs and little bottom…do you remember what to look for to determine the sex?"

"I think I know…" Tyler said.

"Is it a girl?" London asked Joy.

Joy smiled with a nod. "It is a girl."

London stared at the image of her daughter on the screen. Her eyes filled with tears. She had wanted a daughter since she was a little girl, but as she approached her thirties without a life partner in sight, she had started to wonder if it was going to happen for her.

London heard Tyler say, "Maggie..."

She turned her head to look at Tyler. He had tears in his eyes. She hadn't expected that.

"Maggie Brand." She wiped the tears from her cheeks.

Tyler hugged her and kissed her.

"Is that what you're going to name her? Maggie?" Joy cleaned her abdomen. "Do you have a middle name picked out, too?"

"No middle name. Just Maggie Brand," London told her. "My mother's family doesn't give middle names. I don't have a middle name." She looked at Tyler now. "Is that okay?"

"It's okay." Tyler squeezed her hand. "I'm happy."

The two of them walked out of the office, hand in hand, brimming with excitement. Tyler couldn't wait to tell his family, and she wished that she could share the news with her family. She was five months into the pregnancy and she still hadn't told her parents or her son. It was easy to put it off when she was so far away. Even when she video chatted with her son regularly, it was easy for her to hide her baby bump. But she knew that she was running out of time.

"I want to buy something for Maggie before we head home." Tyler said as he opened up the passenger door for her.

They headed to a baby store. There was so much *stuff* for babies that it felt overwhelming.

"You know that Mom has already bought a truck-load of stuff for Maggie, right?"

"I've heard about baby central, but I haven't actually

seen it with my own eyes. I'm a little afraid." London stopped to look at a little pink flouncy dress with pretty white lace accents. "This is adorable."

Tyler picked up the dress, looked at it and smiled. "This is for her first baby picture. We need some shoes, too, don't we?"

London pointed to the other side of the store. "Over there."

They picked out a little pair of white baby shoes for Maggie before they headed back to the ranch. They agreed to tell the family the news when they all gathered for dinner. Tyler headed back out to get some more work done before sunset. She was left alone in the cabin with a new pink baby dress and her own thoughts.

London sat down on the edge of the bed she shared with Tyler and held the perfect little dress in her hands. She started to cry again. The tears were a mixture of happiness and fear. She knew that the news was going to be met with mixed emotions by her family. She didn't want to Maggie to be bad news for anyone, but she would be. Montana had been the fantasy... Virginia was going to be a giant dose of reality.

## Chapter Eleven

When Tyler returned to the cabin that evening, London was sitting on the couch quietly. Normally, the cabin had life when he returned home—music was playing, the lights were on, the furniture had been repositioned. But today was different. It looked different and it *felt* different. Tyler felt his gut tighten. He hung his hat on the hook just inside the door and turned on the light.

"What are you doing sitting in the dark?"

London blinked her eyes several times until they started to adjust to the light. "Thinking."

Tyler sat down next to her. Her body position told a tale—she was sitting on the edge of the couch, elbows on her knees, hands clasped, her head down. Something was wrong and he realized that she had been sitting here, waiting for him, for some time.

"What's going on?" he asked her directly.

A small uncomfortable smile greeted his question, but she didn't look at him. "Tomorrow's the big day."

"I know." As the day for her departure drew closer, his fear started to build. What if she didn't get on the return flight? What would he do then?

"Are you ready?"

She finally looked at him with troubled eyes. "No. I already know how they're going to react. I've been through it once before. Your family has had a chance to adjust to the idea of Maggie. I'm about to blindside mine."

Tyler had been careful not to pry about her communication with her family in Virginia, and London had been careful to call them when he wasn't around. She had always been a private person with a fortress erected protectively around her...but he had to believe that in time he would be able to smash those walls one by one.

"So...you haven't even told your folks?"

"No. This isn't the kind of news you break over the phone."

All day he'd been pushing the thought of London leaving to the back part of his mind. He'd worked long hours and he'd worked hard. But no matter how hard he worked, he couldn't make the odd feeling in the pit of his stomach subside.

London and Maggie had become as important as the land beneath his feet. He couldn't picture a life on the ranch now without them.

"You're coming back." The question he had been wanting to ask ever since she had purchased her plane ticket sounded more like a statement.

London squeezed his hand reassuringly. "Of course.

Of course I'm coming back. You know this is something I need to do, Tyler. I need to go now, before I really start to show."

Tyler had tried to be philosophical about her trip. But the idea that she might decide to stay in Virginia once she got there was always a little demon in the back of his mind. The fact remained, London had not said yes to his marriage proposal. He knew that concern for her son's happiness was at the heart of her refusal to commit to him and to a life on the ranch. It was irrational and misplaced, but he couldn't stop himself from feeling angry toward J.T. It irked him that his fate was in the hands of a twelve-year-old preadolescent.

The two weeks that Tyler spent alone without London felt like the longest weeks of his life. Every day at the ranch, ever since he was a boy, had been a great day. He loved his life. He loved his work. He loved the land. And the ranch had always been enough. But London and his unborn baby had changed that. Now he discovered that he needed them to complete his life at the ranch. In the evening, instead of returning to the lifeless cabin, he spent his time with Luke at the chapel, working on restoring the interior. He wanted to marry London in this chapel before their child was born. Was that a pipe dream?

"Hand me that hammer over there, will you?" Luke's request was the first words they had spoken to each other in nearly an hour.

Tyler grabbed the hammer and handed it off to his brother. Luke wasn't much of a talker, and tonight Tyler didn't feel much like talking. So they worked together in silence, night by night, restoring the floors and the beams and the small altar.

"What's on your mind?" Luke asked out of the blue.

Tyler kept on hand-sanding one of the benches. "Not much."

Luke hammered a nail into place. "You've got a child on the way. No way you don't have that on your mind. You plannin' on marrying her?"

"That's my plan."

Luke stopped hammering and turned to look at him. "Is it her plan?"

It wasn't a barb. Luke wasn't trying to hurt him. He was making an observation and speaking brother to brother.

Tyler dropped his head. "Man to man?"

Luke gave a short nod of agreement. It wouldn't go farther than the walls of the chapel.

"She has a son. A biracial son. I don't care about that, but she's worried that he won't be happy here at the ranch...that he won't fit in. I've told her that Brands take care of Brands, but I can't deny she's got a right to be worried. She shares custody with the father...but the father has made it clear that he wants full custody, so she's afraid she's going to lose her son if she marries me and moves to Montana." It felt good to get this off his chest. "I think we'd be married already if there wasn't another child involved."

Luke wasn't one to answer quickly. He was a man who liked to mull things over before he spoke. After a minute or two, he said, "Are you sure that she's the one you want to marry? Marriage is..." Luke picked up some nails. "Marriage is tough...you got to really love the person, brother. I mean, really love 'em to make it work."

"I love her..." Tyler looked his brother straight in the eye. "I saw her and I thought—*there's my woman. That's my bride.* When she got on that plane..." Tyler turned away from Luke so his brother wouldn't see the moisture gathering in his eyes. "I didn't know I could hurt that much."

The day London was scheduled to return home, Tyler arrived at the airport several hours early. He fidgeted and paced and checked the time on his phone religiously. He felt anxious. Nervous. Impatient. But every negative emotion dissolved like snow on a hot day when he saw London coming down the stairs of the plane. Seeing her, with her long blond hair loose and blowing around her shoulders, he knew that she had worn it down for him. She preferred to keep it off her face and out of her way by braiding it in one thick braid down her back.

When she finally walked through the door and into his arms, Tyler figured out exactly what it meant to be whole. He hadn't felt like himself when London had been away. Would he ever be able to feel normal without her by his side? Like a vital organ in his body...he needed her.

London's heart began to beat wildly in her chest when she spotted Tyler waiting for her in the small airport terminal. It felt as though her heart expanded when she saw him. She had strained to look out the window of the airplane when they landed to try to catch a glimpse of him. And she had stood, impatiently, behind a sweet but slow-moving elderly couple as they tottered slowly toward the exit. It wasn't her general nature, but she cursed them in her mind. She wanted to get down those stairs and get to Tyler as soon as she could, and they were holding up the line!

"Oh, my stars…" Tyler held her face in his hands after her kissed her on the lips. "I have missed you."

"I missed you," London said. She was surprised by how forceful her words sounded. But they were true.

London wrapped her arms around his neck and held him tightly. She had missed his warmth. She had missed his voice. She had missed his kisses.

Tyler leaned back a little and looked down at her rounded belly. She had blossomed recently and she was definitely showing. "How's our girl?"

"Busy! *Very* busy." London linked her arm with his.

"And your family?"

London shook her head. "Let's not talk about that just yet. Okay? I want to enjoy being home with you."

The lovemaking that night was slow and tender. They both wanted to savor the reunion…make it last. Afterward, they held each other, grateful to be back together. Unfortunately, the tender moment was interrupted by a horrendous calf cramp.

"Oooow! Ow! Ow! *Ow!*" London shot upright and made a grab for her lower leg.

"What?" Tyler switched on the light.

"Leg cramp! I can't reach it. My belly's in the way!" London tried again to reach it.

"I got it." Tyler stood up and took her right leg in his hands. "I got it. Lie back."

Tyler's hands were strong from a lifetime spent on the ranch. He massaged her calf muscle until he felt her begin to relax.

"Better?" he asked.

She nodded with relief. "Why are you so good to me?"

Tyler laughed a small laugh. He lay down in the bed beside her, his head near her feet. He took her bare feet into his hands and began to massage them.

"One...you deserve it." He wiggled her little toe. "Two...I love you." He wiggled another toe. "And three...my mom and sisters would castrate me if I didn't."

He loved the way London laughed and tried to get her to do it as often as possible. Luckily, she thought he was funny and he could make her laugh easily.

"Oh!" London put her hand on her rounded abdomen.

"Too hard?" Tyler stopped massaging her feet.

"No... Maggie just kicked the bejesus out of me! I hope she doesn't have my Sasquatch feet!"

"I like your feet."

"Please..." London shook her head with a frown. "I was called Lurch all throughout high school. That made me popular with all the boys." She held up her hands. "I have man hands."

"Well...I think you're beautiful."

"I think you're handsome." London returned the compliment.

They lazed in bed together for another hour until they were driven to the kitchen by their hunger. Tyler had prepared for her return by stocking the refrigerator with her favorite craving foods that didn't activate her overly sensitive olfactory system. They went out to the deck that overlooked the lake. It was one of their favorite places to be together.

London hunched her shoulders a little. "The temperature's actually dropped a little since I've been gone."

"We're heading into fall now." Tyler brought his cup of coffee up to his mouth to blow on the piping-hot liquid.

She felt as if she was home when she was at Bent Tree. But after the two emotional weeks she had just experienced with her family back east, she couldn't predict whether or not she had a future on the ranch.

Tyler had been watching London closely. Her face, such a pretty face to his eyes, had just displayed a myriad of emotions. She hadn't wanted to talk about her visit home, but he couldn't wait any longer.

"What happened when you went home?" When she avoided answering his question about her family at the airport, he knew that it couldn't be good news. "How did they react?"

London looked away and tried to suppress a rush of tears.

"Obviously it didn't go well…" Tyler added.

"No…" London crossed her arms in front of her body. "It didn't go well."

Everything about London's body language changed when he brought up her trip. Her shoulders slumped, her mouth thinned and the displeasure in her light blue eyes told a story that her words had yet to say.

Tyler cared for her, so he cared about the reaction of her entire family. But the one that truly counted was the reaction of her son.

"What about J.T.?"

"Really angry."

It was understandable that her son was angry. They had made a deal—her degree meant that they could finally move out of her parents' house and get their own place together. Ever since J.T. was born, they had been like the two musketeers. She had been a young, single mother on her own; they had struggled in the early years and that struggle had bonded them.

"But," she continued, "he's willing to give Montana a shot...for me."

"Then I'm going to do everything I can to make sure J.T. loves the ranch," Tyler assured her. "And if there's one thing the Brands are good at, it's making folks feel at home."

The day after Thanksgiving marked London's sixth month. She was showing now and didn't feel the need to try to hide it any longer. The stress of keeping a secret was gone, but the stress of introducing her son to the ranch, and vice versa, was still hard to manage. Whenever they spoke on the phone, her mom was quick to point out all of the financial burdens they were carrying—from house payments to medical bills, her parents had been underwater for a long time. She knew that the child support wasn't enough to cover all of J.T.'s expenses, and even though she sent half of the money she made working on the ranch to her parents, it still wasn't enough to feed a growing boy. Her father always had an *I told you so* tone of voice during their rare phone calls. He had speculated that she would find a way to self-sabotage this degree as well. The only positive conversations she had postconfession were with her stepfather. He was the one parent she could always count on to cheer her on no matter what.

And now, when she video chatted with her son, she could see on his face the disappointment and resentment. He didn't want to leave his friends, his basketball team, his life. That's why he hadn't wanted to go live with his father in the first place. Montana might as well be on Mars, it seemed so alien and remote to J.T.

She felt grateful that she had Sophia to lift her spirits. And there was always something that needed to be done on the ranch. Today, the day after Thanksgiving, it was time to begin decorating the ranch for Christmas. Barbara had a steadfast tradition—she put up her Christmas decorations the day after Thanksgiving and took them down, without fail, the first day of the New Year.

"Is this box too heavy for you?" Sophia pointed to box near her leg.

They were in the attic searching for the Christmas boxes.

"No way." London picked up the box without any difficulty. She had always been just as strong as most of the boys, and sometimes even stronger.

"Thanks for helping." Sophia picked up one of the boxes labeled X-MAS. "Mom already has enough to worry about with Dad's health. I'd like to just take care of all of this holiday stuff for her."

"I'm glad to help. I've always loved Christmas… ornaments, carols, lights, wrapping presents. My mom worked nights as a waitress and there was never a lot of money, so our Christmases were always on a shoestring budget. I would look at the houses in the neighborhood that had lights up with so much envy. I've never been able to give my son the Christmas I've wanted to give him. Of course, he gets really expensive gifts from his father. But I mean the picture-perfect Christmas with a real tree, mistletoe, eggnog, caroling…the whole bit."

"Well…" Sophia put her box on the kitchen table.

"You've come to the right place, then. The Brand family will pull out all the stops, especially since your son is visiting. I know Hank is planning on waiting to find the Christmas tree until after J.T. arrives."

London shook her head in amazement, her hands on top of the closed box. "Barb and Hank are too good to be true."

"You would think." Sophia took the first Christmas decoration out of the box and began to carefully unwrap it. "But I've known them for years and they've never changed. They're just good people."

They unpacked the boxes quietly for a moment. Over the past several weeks, she had become close with Sophia. In fact, she would count Sophia among her friends.

"Do you mind if I pry a little?" Sophia asked her.

"Not really…"

Sophia was quick to add, "If it's too personal, just say so, and I'll completely understand."

"I feel like everyone already knows all of my business here. How personal could it really be?"

Sophia laughed. "You're right. It's hard to have privacy with this family."

"So…what do you want to know?"

"Well…" Sophia stopped unpacking. "I was just wondering, why don't you have a ring on your finger? It's obvious in the way he looks at you that Tyler adores you…and you seem to love him. You're having a baby together… Don't you want to get married?"

When London didn't respond immediately, Sophia went back to unpacking with a sheepish shake of her head. "Too personal, right? I'm sorry… Luke always tells me I'm too nosy. Just please forgive me and forget I asked, okay?"

At first, London did think that the question was too personal. But Sophia had a way about her. She was easy to talk to. So she decided to take a chance and trust her—open up to her. She shared her worries about her son and the difficulties ahead. Her son's father was already lawyered up, and she had never been able to compete with his finances.

"Yeah…but it's different now." Sophia put the empty box to the side. "You have the Brands behind you. Everything's changed. Trust me. And you're right—money does make the difference when the person on the other side can afford the fees. But it's hard to have deeper pockets than Hank and Barb. They don't flaunt it, but you'd better believe that they've got it."

London sat down, surveying their work. "I just wish that it was easier. That I could just say yes to Tyler without a second thought." She ran her hand over the large snowman candle. "But I have J.T. And trust me…he's a city kind of kid. His dream is to go to college in a big city like Chicago or New York. Montana is the exact *opposite* of what he wants. Well…you know. You're moving here from Boston."

Sophia sat down at the table as well. "I totally get your son. I prefer skyscrapers to mountain views any day of the week."

Everyone had been shocked by Luke's announcement that he was moving his family back to Montana. But Sophia and Luke hadn't really given a specific reason for their radical decision.

"Now it's my turn to pry," she said to Sophia. "Why in the world would you leave Boston? Tyler told me that you have a successful practice there…and you obviously love it."

Sophia tucked a honey-colored strand of hair behind her ear. "You confided in me, so it's only fair that I confide in you. Luke was diagnosed with PTSD."

"Oh… I'm really sorry to hear that."

"I suppose I've always known. But it took Luke a while to accept it…to go and get diagnosed officially by a doctor at the VA."

London had a friend who had done one too many tours in Iraq. "How many tours did he do?"

"Four," Sophia said, a wrinkle forming in her forehead. "He deployed four times to Afghanistan…" She met London's eyes. "He's always on guard, always on alert. With all of the noises and people and stimulation… Luke can't live in a big city." Sophia shrugged one shoulder. "And I can't live without him."

Sophia and Luke were as bonded as two people could be. Opposites, yes, but devoted nonetheless. London wanted that kind of love…that kind of marriage. And she believed, without reservation, that she could have it with Tyler.

## Chapter Twelve

J.T. arrived on a Tuesday, the morning after a heavy snowfall. The landscape resembled a winter wonderland—the white, white snow was sparkling as the light from the warm sun brushed over it. It was cold…really cold. And that worried London. J.T. wasn't a fan of the cold, and winters in Montana could be brutal. In fact, London knew that a Montana winter would make a Virginia winter seem like child's play in comparison. London had brought extra outerwear for J.T. to put on at the airport, just in case the clothing he wore on the plane wasn't warm enough to protect him from the freezing temperatures.

She had chewed her thumbnail to the quick awaiting her son's arrival. When she saw him getting off the plane, she had to fight back the tears. At the entrance to the airport, London hugged her son tightly and kissed him on his cold cheek. Tyler hung back, respecting the mother and son reunion.

London put her arm around J.T.'s shoulders and pulled him closer to her. He resisted a little, which let her know that he was still unhappy about Montana *and* the baby. But she kept him close to her despite his subtle protest.

"How are you?" she asked him.

"Cold," J.T. replied sullenly.

"Me, too," she agreed. There was no sense denying the fact that it was ridiculously cold. "I'm glad you're here."

J.T. didn't respond verbally, but his downturned mouth and tiny shake of his head let her know, in no uncertain terms, that her feeling was not mutual. As they walked toward Tyler, London knew that they had a very steep hill to climb in order for J.T. to feel at home in big sky country.

Tyler's first impression of J.T. was that he carried himself in a way that made him seem to be much older than his twelve years. He was a good-looking kid with intelligent brown eyes—and tall. He was nearly as tall as London already, which meant he was almost six feet tall. His face was a little chubby and he appeared to be carrying some extra weight. His vacation on Bent Tree would slim him down if he didn't overindulge in all of the Christmas cookies, cakes and hot chocolate Barb would be pushing.

The meeting between her son and the man she wanted to marry was a simple uneventful greeting. They shook hands, said hello and then focused on the tasks of getting J.T.'s suitcase and heading to the truck. J.T. didn't have much to say on the trip to the ranch. He sat in the backseat with his headphones plugged in to his ears. Tyler didn't have much to say, either—but she knew that he was tense inside by the way his fingers were gripping the steering wheel and the way he kept on glancing at J.T. in the rearview mirror. Tyler was worried and so was she.

"Hey…" London caught a glimpse of J.T.'s phone for the first time. "When did you get that?"

"When I was with Dad."

"He got you an iPhone?" London had a constant battle with Jon about how they should raise their son. She didn't think that J.T. was old enough to have an expensive phone.

"He's paying for it."

She knew exactly what her son was intimating—Jon was paying for the phone, so why should she care one way or the other? But she did care. It was the principle of the thing. And Jon knew that she didn't want J.T. to have an iPhone yet, and so did her son, for that matter.

"That's not the point." She turned forward in her seat. "We'll talk about it later."

She didn't want to start off J.T.'s time in Montana on a bad note, but she couldn't abandon all of her principles in an attempt to win him over. He was a smart kid. He'd be expecting her to do that. He might even be banking on it.

"I don't know what the big deal is," J.T. answered back. "He just wants to be able to see me when we talk. Like you do."

The last time Jon had bought their son an iPhone, J.T. was ten years old and she had sent the phone back to him.

"We'll talk about it later," she repeated. She wanted

J.T. to be happy and she wanted him to have the things he wanted. But she didn't want him to be spoiled or entitled like so many kids of his generation were. She wanted him to know the value of hard work, of saving money and earning his own way. Jon, on the other hand, wanted J.T. to have all the material things that he hadn't been able to have when he was a boy. Jon didn't want his son to struggle.

When they arrived at the ranch, a light snow had started to fall. J.T. climbed out of the truck and looked all around at the ranch with a look of disappointment on his face.

"Where are your neighbors?" J.T. asked.

Tyler opened the covered bed of his truck to get J.T.'s suitcase. "We don't have any."

"That's what I love about the ranch," London chimed in. "No neighbors."

"I like neighbors," J.T. muttered. "You didn't tell me we'd be way out in the boonies."

London ignored her son's bitterness. "Come on…let's drop your bag off in your room and then go to the main house. Tyler's family is waiting to meet you."

Like any normal kid, J.T. could be grouchy and disagreeable, but for the most part, he'd always been a pretty easygoing boy. Today, though, he seemed determined to be dissatisfied with everything and everyone. London reminded him, quietly and firmly, to be polite to Tyler's family when he met them. She understood that he was ticked off, but being rude to the Brands was unacceptable.

At the main house, London couldn't have asked for a warmer welcome for her son. Hank, who typically wouldn't be at the main house at this time of day, was in the kitchen with Barb and Danny. Luke and Sophia had been playing blocks with their toddlers in the family room. But when they came through the front door, bringing a blast of frigid air with them into the foyer, Luke and Sophia each picked up a twin so they could greet them.

Everyone was in the foyer now, including Ilsa, the German shepherd, and Ranger, the family's sociable black cat. The main house felt hot inside with their heavy outerwear holding the heat to their bodies. The three of them started to shed their jackets and gloves and hats while the introductions were made. J.T. didn't really have time to be negative because Tyler's mom invited him into the kitchen for some hot chocolate with marshmallows.

"Are you hungry?" Barb asked J.T.

He was always hungry.

"Yes, ma'am."

Barbara brought a cookie jar over to the table. "I heard these are your favorite."

J.T. looked inside the cookie jar to find freshly baked oatmeal-raisin cookies. London saw her son's eyes light up.

"Take as many as you want," Barb told him. "They're homemade just for you."

J.T. looked at his mom. London nodded her head. "Special occasion."

Her son said thank you to Barb after he created a fortress of cookies in front of him. This was the perfect way for J.T. to meet Tyler's family.

"Thank you for this." London reached over her son's shoulders and stole the top cookie from the pile. "Mmm. These are really good. Family recipe?"

"Grandma Brand. Maggie was an amazing cook."

"I'm going to get some work done." Tyler stood next to her. He had been very reluctant to touch her in front of her son. "Is that okay with you?"

"Sure. We'll see you for dinner?"

"Dinner," Tyler confirmed.

London knew that Tyler always had work to do, but he was escaping. He was uncomfortable with her son and he was retreating.

Hank sat down at the table with J.T., his hand, as always, petting Ilsa's graying head. "You ever cut down a Christmas tree?"

J.T., mouth full of cookie, shook his head. He chewed quickly so he could swallow and answer. "My dad had a real Christmas tree one year, but Shelly didn't like cleaning up after it, so he never had one again. We always have a fake tree."

"We need to find our tree—we've been waiting on you," Hank told him. "I need you to help Danny and me pick out the tree, cut it down and haul it back here so we can decorate it."

J.T. had a really close bond with all of his grandparents. London had always thought that he was an old soul because he liked to hang out with his grandmother and play Scrabble for hours. Even though he hadn't connected with Tyler, it was clear that he was immediately drawn to no-nonsense Hank.

"No heavy lifting," Barb reminded her husband. "Doctor's orders."

Hank reached out for his wife's hand, caught it and kissed it. "J.T. and Luke can do the hard work. I'll supervise."

Danny climbed up into Hank's lap. "Let's get the twee…"

Sophia put down her wiggling daughter with a little laugh. "I think Danny's ready for the Christmas tree."

"Me, too," London said.

For the past several weeks they had been decorating the inside of the house. All of the Brand family decorations were unpacked and put in their designated places. Barbara had collected glass gingerbread houses and miniature Christmas trees with twinkling lights, Santa Clauses of different sizes, fancy holiday candles, candy dishes full of holiday candy, and mistletoe. Stockings were hung. The house had been transformed from a farmhouse to a holiday house. The men had put up the lights on the outside of the house as well as some of the trees nearby. But for all the holiday spirit that had been infused into the house, there was a glaring hole where the tree would sit in the family room near the fireplace. They needed the tree to have a place to put all of the wrapped presents. And there were a ton. It was going to be a very merry Christmas this year.

J.T. took his cup and plate over to Barbara. He stood quietly until she looked up at him. "Oh…just put them on the counter there. I'll take care of them."

Hank stood up as well. He studied J.T.'s red Air Jordan basketball shoes for a minute. "You got boots?"

"No, sir."

Hank made eye contact with Barbara. "We're going to have to get this young man some boots."

"Tyler and I were going to take him to town…get him a hat and some boots," London assured him.

"Well…" Hank pulled one of his hats off the hat rack and plopped it on J.T.'s head. "This'll have to do until you get one of your own. Here…" He held out one of his thick, wool-lined coats. "Try this on for size."

J.T. slipped on the coat. The sleeves were a little long and the waist a little loose, but overall, it fit pretty well.

"Do you drive?" Hank asked her son.

For the first time since he had arrived in Montana, her son smiled. It was a brief flicker of a smile, but she saw it. Held on to it.

"No. I'm twelve."

"Luke here started to drive when he was eight."

"That's true…" Luke was kneeling in front of little Danny, buttoning up his coat.

"We'll have to get you behind the wheel while you're here." Hank shrugged on his coat and grabbed his favorite hat.

J.T. didn't say anything, but the word *cool* was written all over his face. Thank goodness for Hank! He'd managed to break the ice with her son in record time. He hadn't asked J.T. if he wanted to go get the Christmas tree—he had stated it as a fact. J.T. hadn't been given the chance to say no to the idea, and that was exactly the right thing for Hank to do. While Hank and the boys went to find their Christmas tree, London went to find Tyler. She needed to make sure he was okay.

"Hi…" She found him in the main barn, checking on a new calf that had been born sickly.

"Hi." It was so cold, but Tyler was sweating from working in the barn.

"Do I get a hug?" she asked him.

Tyler wiped the sweat from his brow with a smile. "I'll give you more than that."

When she stepped into his arms, he kissed her… It was a sweet, tender kiss, full of promise. Had she been holding her breath, wondering if he would change now that her son was at the ranch? She hadn't realized that was what she had been doing until he kissed her.

"Hmm...nice." She smiled up at him.

"Did you like that?"

"Uh-huh."

He kissed her again. This time, the kiss was deeper and longer... It was the kind of kiss that started that tingling sensation between her thighs.

"I like you," Tyler murmured after the kiss.

She snuggled closer to his body for warmth with a smile. About the calf, she asked, "How is she?"

Tyler shook his head, his eyes concerned. "It never fails that we have calves drop on the coldest nights. I'm not altogether sure that she's going to survive."

"Oh..." London was drawn to the stall gate. "No. She has to make it. You have to save her."

Tyler joined her at the gate. "I'm gonna give it my best shot."

London nodded. She knew that he would. Tyler was a champion of the newborns on the ranch. It was his passion to see that they survived. With a shiver, she turned away from the calf.

"I'm freezing out here."

Tyler put his arm around her. "Why don't you go back on inside? I'll meet you back at the house."

London gave him another quick kiss before she turned to walk away. She took a couple of steps but stopped. She turned back to him.

"Hank seems to have a way with J.T."

Tyler was pulling on his work gloves. "I noticed that. That's good."

London nodded as she thought about how to formulate what was on her mind. After a quiet second or two, she asked, "Do you think that you and J.T. will be able to…make a connection?"

Tyler walked over to her. "Look, don't stress yourself out worrying about that. It's not good for you or the baby. You let me handle it."

"Okay," She agreed. "But…"

He shook his head, put his hands on her shoulders, spun her around and gave her a gentle nudge in the other direction.

"It's gonna just take a little time, but your son and I will find our footing with each other."

Tyler was done talking about it—she knew that. So she went back to the main house to see if she could help Barb and Sophia with dinner. Dinner was under control, but the toddler twins were not. London wrangled spunky little Abigail, while Sophia corralled Annabelle. They spent the next hour entertaining the twins until it was time for them to go down for a nap. As they were coming down the stairs, the door swung open. Hank stomped his boots on the mat outside the door before he came in. She saw J.T. follow his example, as did little four-year-old Danny. Luke was the last to come in out of the cold.

"Darlin'!" Hank called out to his wife.

Barb appeared from the back of the house. "Did you find one?"

"Did we find one!" Hank's voice boomed. She hadn't seen him this animated since before his mild heart attack. "You're not dealing with amateurs!"

London and Sophia joined them in the foyer.

"J.T. and Danny found us a beautiful ten-footer," Hank bragged proudly.

Luke gave Sophia a hug and kiss, then started to take off his winter gear.

"Come here, my big boy." Sophia unbuttoned Danny's coat. "Did you find us a Christmas tree?"

Danny nodded his head happily.

"I'm going to take him upstairs and get him out of these wet clothes," Sophia told them.

J.T. didn't have much of a smile on his face. London asked him, "Did you have a good time?"

J.T. glanced at Hank, who was out of earshot. "It was okay."

"Just okay?" She bumped her shoulder to his.

Her son nodded.

All right. So he was determined to minimize the experience. But she knew better. J.T. had always asked for a real Christmas tree. To be able to actually go out in the forest and cut down his own tree? He might not want to admit it, but *that* was an experience of a lifetime.

"Go wash up for dinner," she told her son. "Down this hallway—second door on the left."

Tyler returned to the main house and they all sat down at the dinner table in the kitchen. The long table made to seat a small army of ranch hands was filling up for the holidays. J.T. was a quiet, focused eater. He went back for seconds of chicken and had four glasses of Barbara's famous homemade root beer. After dinner, they cleaned the kitchen and prepared to bring the large fir tree into the house. They had left the tree on the porch in a large bucket of water to stop it from drying out.

"Please make sure that there aren't any critters in that tree before you bring it into the house," Barb said from the doorway. "I don't need a mouse or bugs in here."

It took Luke, Tyler, Hank and J.T. to bring the fluffy

dark green fir tree into the house. Sophia and London prepared the space in the family room where the tree would live for the holiday season. Once the tree was in its place, they put the ornaments on the coffee table and took the strings of lights out of their boxes.

"I have a stocking," J.T. told his mom.

London smiled at him. "I saw that."

"This is my favorite part of the whole season!" Barb exclaimed.

"If you're happy, then I'm happy." Hank kissed his wife on the cheek before he sneaked off to bed.

"Are you ready?" Sophia asked her husband. She held out the lights to him. Luke always manned the lights—he was patient enough to string the lights in a perfectly symmetrical pattern.

Barb turned on Christmas carols and London started to sing quietly along to some of her favorite holiday tunes. She could never really sing well, but she loved Christmas carols. There was safety in numbers.

After Luke finished stringing the lights, he sat down while the rest of the family hung the ornaments. They filled the beautiful fir tree with colored crystal balls, red velvet bows and hand-painted wooden ornaments with moving parts that Barb had collected over the years.

"Hank usually likes to put the star on the tree, but I think he'd want you to do it this year." Barb held the delicate glass star in her hands.

J.T. smiled at Tyler's mom with his eyes, even though it didn't reach his lips. He climbed up onto a sturdy step stool and carefully placed the star on the top of the tree. When he climbed off the stool, Sophia turned off the lights and they all admired the twinkling Christmas tree.

"That's the most beautiful Christmas tree I've ever seen." London had her hand resting on her stomach. The baby was kicking her. "And it smells so good."

"I love the smell of a Christmas tree," Barb agreed.

London was grateful that her olfactory system could handle the strong smell of the tree. It wouldn't do to be sick every time she got near the tree.

"You owe me a kiss," Tyler whispered in her ear.

She looked at him and followed his eyes upward. She was standing beneath the mistletoe.

Before she kissed him, she did glance at her son, who was looking down at his phone now. She gave Tyler a quick kiss, feeling uncomfortable with the idea of showing affection to Tyler in front of J.T. He'd never seen her with a man—she rarely dated and hadn't liked any man enough to bring him home to meet her son.

"Merry Christmas." Tyler stood behind her, his hands on her shoulders.

"Merry Christmas," she said, forcing herself to unstiffen her shoulders when he touched her.

Looking at that elegant tree, so perfectly dressed for the holidays with bright red bows and twinkling white lights, London did have hope that it would be a merry Christmas…for her *and* for her son.

## Chapter Thirteen

"Where's J.T.?" A cold blast of night air followed Tyler inside the warm cabin when he walked through the front door. Tyler had gone over to the main house to talk to his father. He didn't take long, but when he returned, only London was sitting in the living room in front of the fire.

"He went to bed." London was sitting on the floor, leaning back against one of the chairs, her legs curled to the side. "Your father has him getting up so early and working so hard, he can't hardly keep his eyes open through dinner."

She had wanted Tyler and her son to bond—in order for her life to fall neatly into place, she actually *needed* them to bond. But her son hadn't bonded with Tyler— he had bonded with Hank and ranch hand Clint McCallister and ranch foreman Brock McCallister. It seemed as if her son had bonded with quite a few people and animals on the ranch…but not the one person she really had wanted him to get to know. Her son's winter break from school was short—every day counted, especially since blended families could take years to jell. They only had *weeks* to at least get some bonding accomplished between the three—soon to be four—of them.

"It's starting to snow again." Tyler unzipped his thick fleece coat and Ranger's black head poked out. Tyler put the cat down on the floor before he got out of his wet coat and boots.

"Hey, Ranger…" London reached out to rub her hand over the big coal-black cat's back.

Ranger greeted her with his signature chatter. Then he lay down in front of the fireplace to give himself a bath.

Tyler leaned down to give her a kiss with lips still cold from the outside. He asked her, "Another log?"

"Please."

Tyler hunkered down and stacked a couple of logs on the fire. London watched her cowboy. There were so many things she had grown to love about him, beyond the physical. She loved how he never tired of getting a rise out of his mom—and when he succeeded, he would glance at her with a small mischievous smile and a wink. She loved how he genuinely cared about the animals on the ranch and how he respected the land that had been passed down in his family for generations. And she loved how he showed her, every day, in little thoughtful ways, that he loved her and their unborn child. Tyler Brand was a romantic man, in his own way. It wasn't about flowers and candy for him. It was adding another log on the fire, or pulling out her chair when she sat down, or surprising her with a horse-drawn buggy ride. That kind of romance suited her just fine.

Tyler joined her on the rug. He put his arm around her shoulder and she turned her body in to his. She leaned her head on his shoulder, pressed her nose into his neck.

"You have the best-smelling skin of any person I've ever known." She breathed in his scent. "I love the way you smell."

Tyler pulled her closer to him. "I'm glad."

They sat together in silence, enjoying the quiet of the night and the heat of the fire on the bottoms of their bare feet. Ranger, his fur hot from the fire, walked on top of Tyler's long, outstretched legs to curl up in his lap.

This was her idea of a perfect night. The baby inside her belly was taking a break from moving around so much and she was snuggled up with her man, listening to the sounds of his breath and the crackling of the fire and the low rumble of Ranger's loud purring. Her son was asleep in the room down the hall. Perfect.

"I told Dad to let J.T. sleep in tomorrow morning," Tyler said after a bit. "He's been borrowing boots and hats for too long. Let's take him in to town tomorrow and get him some of his own gear."

London had slipped her hand beneath Tyler's shirt. She had a favorite little trail of hair on his stomach that she liked to run her fingers over while she was in his arms. She turned her head upward with a smile.

"I'd like that," she said, then added a moment later, "You haven't really had much time with J.T."

She was worried. He heard it in her voice. "It's going to work out between J.T. and me."

She pushed herself upright so she could look into his

face. "How do you know? The two of you have hardly said more than ten words to each other. Tops."

He pulled her back in to his arms, kissed the top of her head. "I just know."

"But...*how* do you know?"

"I feel it," he told her. "I can't explain it."

"Try..."

"Do you know how you felt when you saw Rising Sun run in the field for the first time? You told me that you knew instantly that he was going to be a champion. How did you know?"

She shrugged one shoulder. "I saw something in him."

"Something special," Tyler added.

"That's right."

"Something intangible..."

"Yes."

"I saw something in your son when I first met him," Tyler told her.

London sat up, spun around to face Tyler, her back to the fire. They hadn't really talked about her son since he had arrived in Montana—she was thirsty for any sign that Tyler *liked* J.T.

"He's got cowboy in his blood," Tyler continued. "When I saw that, I knew that he was going to make it on the ranch. Dad must've seen it, too, or he wouldn't have taken him under his wing like he did."

London picked at a fray in the hand-woven rug. "J.T. already thinks the sun rises and sets with Hank."

Tyler nodded.

"But...that doesn't mean he's going to want to live here," London said. "What if..."

He took her fidgeting hand into his. "Hey…what needs to happen is happening already."

"But he doesn't talk to you…he hardly talks to me. Why are you so optimistic?"

"Because…" Tyler moved Ranger off his lap and guided her back into his arms. "He's already got Montana air in his lungs."

"Hmm." London let herself relax back into his strong arms. She believed Bent Tree was a magical place. It had certainly worked its magic on her. Did her son feel it, too?

Tyler tilted her chin up so he could kiss her. His kisses were so tender, so sensual. He liked to take his time, linger on her mouth and massage her aching, swollen breasts with his strong hands. He always wanted to make her feel better…he always wanted to please her.

"J.T. could wake up," London whispered against Tyler's exploring lips.

"Then let's go into the bedroom."

Tyler had taken to sleeping on the couch ever since J.T. arrived. Even after J.T. had fallen asleep, she hadn't been able to bring herself to make love with Tyler with her son in the house. She was always worried that he would wake up and discover them.

"Okay," she agreed. She had to learn how to be with Tyler, as his woman, as his wife, with her son under the same roof. If they were going to become a family, she had to learn to relax and try to behave how she would normally behave with Tyler.

Tyler took her hand and led her into the bedroom. He shut the door and locked it. They met each other under the blankets, their naked skin hot from the fire. The sheets were cold and London squirmed until her back was pressed tightly against his naked chest and torso. She had unbraided her freshly washed hair, still damp, before she had gotten into bed. Tyler liked the feel of her long hair on his skin. He loved to wrap himself up in it, run his fingers through it…smell it.

"I love you," he murmured against her neck. "You make me so happy."

"You make me happy."

She turned in his arms so she could kiss him in the dark.

"Lie back."

They had begun to know each other as lovers. She knew what he wanted with this simple command. She sank back into the pillows. Tyler wanted to love her all the time. He found the changes in her body, as her belly grew with his seed, sexy.

Her eyes closed, she moaned when his mouth closed over her nipple. Her breasts were so sore and swollen now, but his constant attention with his hands and his lips had helped relieve some of the tenderness.

"Oh…" She threaded her fingers into his hair and pressed down. "God."

Tyler suckled her breast until she signaled to him that she needed more. He moved his attention downward to the lower part of her body, dropping butterfly kisses on her rounded belly until he was positioned between her thighs.

Tyler made her feel desirable. He made her feel wanted. And he made her body feel so very good, it was hard now to imagine a time in her pregnancy when she *wouldn't* want Tyler to love her.

London turned her head to the pillow and bit her lip to stop herself from crying out when Tyler's tongue slipped inside her body. His hands underneath her hips, he lifted her up higher so he could have her for dessert.

"You taste so sweet," Tyler told her.

He always pushed her to the edge. He was patient, persistent...he feasted on her until she couldn't be still, until she was clutching the sheets, her back was arched and she was writhing against his mouth.

"What do you want?" he asked her as he kissed the inside of her thigh.

*"You..."*

Tyler turned her over, pulled her hips backward toward him and entered her from behind. Her head dropped down and all she wanted to do was enjoy the sensation of Tyler's hard, thick shaft stroking in and out of her body. Long, deliberate, sensual strokes meant to please her. And they did. But she wanted more. She surprised him by slipping her body away from his. She pushed on his chest.

"Lie back."

When she had him on his back, she climbed on top of him and took him for a ride. This was the position she liked the best. It was so easy to take charge, to know the right angle and the right depth. It was so easy to pleasure her body this way.

Tyler pulled her forward and captured her nipple in his mouth. He sucked on her nipple hard. He knew her well enough to know exactly what he needed to do to help her reach her climax. When he felt her begin to crest, he joined her, pumping his shaft into her hot core, faster and harder, until he grabbed her hips, pushed her down and strained upward with a deep, satisfied groan.

She collapsed onto his chest with a laugh. Loving Tyler had become a bit of an art form. It never got old.

It never got boring. It was just as exciting and satisfying now as it had been in the beginning. Maybe even more because they knew each other's bodies so well.

"Are you okay?"

After that one time when she had started to have contractions after lovemaking, Tyler was always concerned.

"I'm great." She kissed him. "How are you?"

"I'm with you."

She fell asleep in Tyler's arms. She knew that he would get up some time before dawn, while it was still dark in the cabin, and return to the couch. He respected her relationship with her son and she could count on him to not get caught in bed with her until they were married.

Tyler was certain that things were set in stone...that J.T. had cowboy in his blood. But she wasn't so sure. If she could get him to take the earbuds out for a second when they were together, maybe she could gauge his mood. But if he wasn't with Hank, he was completely absorbed with listening to music or watching videos on his phone. Where was her son's head really at right now? She wished, as his mother, that it were easier to know. Why did it seem, now that he was almost a teenager, she was starting to be one of the *last* to know?

J.T. looked at himself in the mirror. "This one."

Tyler was standing next to him holding two Stetsons. J.T. had a dark brown Stetson on his head and a new pair of cowboy boots on his feet. Dressed in jeans and a plaid shirt, with a Western belt and buckle, her boy looked much more like a rancher and a lot less like the urban kid who had stepped off the plane wearing basketball shoes.

"I like that one the best, too," she agreed.

"All right." Tyler nodded. To the sales clerk, he said, "We'll take this hat, the boots and the belt."

It was a strange thing to watch Tyler with her son. They didn't have much to say to each other, but they appeared to be much more comfortable around each other. It was as if they had found some sort of unspoken balance together. And it occurred to her that they were actually pretty similar people, and perhaps that's why their approach to their relationship appeared odd to the person outside it.

"You've lost some weight." London admired her handsome son.

J.T. had always had a weight problem. He'd been a superchubby baby, a husky toddler and a heavyset preteen. She knew he got teased at school because of it, even though he didn't talk about it much.

He had noticed it, too, and she could tell that he liked what he saw—he actually smiled when he looked at himself in the mirror. He was tall for his age, and now he was slimming down and filling out with some muscle.

"Hank's been working me hard," J.T. told her. "I'm sore all over."

Tyler walked over to them with a receipt in his hand. He handed J.T. the bag.

"We're set here," he said to them.

"Thank you." London put her hand on Tyler's arm. It was a sweet thing he had done, setting J.T. up with a cowboy uniform. He had his own boots and hat now. He was official.

"Yeah..." J.T. addressed Tyler for once. "Thanks."

"I'm glad to do it," Tyler told them. "You're a rancher now."

As they walked together, as a trio, through historic Helena, London noticed the looks that her son was drawing. Her son hadn't always been received the way she would have expected, and she knew she was hypersensitive to it because he had been picked on before for being biracial. There was still some prejudice in the country. There was still some prejudice in her own family…with her own father. But even though J.T. was receiving some looks, they weren't *hateful* looks. And there weren't a lot. Certainly not as many as she had thought there would be. And J.T. didn't seem to notice or care one way or the other.

"I want to do a little Christmas shopping with J.T.," Tyler told her. "How 'bout I drop you off at the baby store with my credit card?"

It didn't take much to bribe her. She wasn't much of a shopper, but the idea of being turned loose in a baby store to shop for her daughter? That was *very* enticing. Little girls were the best to shop for!

Tyler and J.T. didn't have much to say to each other in the truck. J.T. listened to his music and Tyler drove. When he got to his destination, Tyler pulled into a spot and turned off the engine. He looked over at J.T. Now was as good a time as any.

"I want to talk to you about something, J.T."

J.T. pulled his earbuds out of his ears.

"Christmas is almost here." Tyler leaned on the steering wheel. "I want to put a ring under the tree for your mom."

When J.T. didn't say anything, Tyler added, "I want to ask your mom to marry me."

"Yeah…I figured," J.T. said noncommittally.

"I want to marry her before your sister is born." Tyler looked over at the preteen. "How would you feel about that?"

J.T.'s face was blank. "I don't know. I have to think about it, I suppose."

"That's fair." Tyler leaned back. "Let's go in this store right here while you think about it."

Friends of the family owned the jewelry store, and Tyler knew that he would be able to find a ring for London here. They carried beautiful and rare pieces that were as beautiful and rare as London was to him.

"Tyler!" The owner came out from behind the display case to shake his hand. "Merry Christmas!"

"Merry Christmas." Tyler shook his hand. "Business's booming."

"'Tis the season." The owner smiled.

"This is J.T." Tyler introduced the two. "He's visiting from Virginia."

"Nice to meet you, J.T." The jeweler stuck out his hand again. "Are you cold enough?"

"I guess." London's son turned back into the shy kid he had met at the airport.

"So…what brings you in? A little Christmas shopping?"

Tyler nodded.

"Well," the jeweler said, "you caught me at the right time. I just finished with my last customer when you walked in the door. What can I do you for?"

"I'm looking for an engagement ring."

"An engagement ring? Usually news like that travels."

"Well…" Tyler followed the man over to the cases. "I can keep a secret."

The owner went behind the cases where the engagement rings were housed. "Who's the lucky lady?"

"J.T.'s mother." Tyler took off his hat and put it on the counter.

"Well, then…you can help us pick out the ring for her. Which one would your mom like?"

J.T. looked into the case. He took his time, examining each one carefully. Finally he pointed. "That one."

J.T. had selected an emerald-cut natural emerald surrounded by diamonds on a high mount.

The owner pulled the ring out of the case, polished it, looked at the price tag, then handed it to Tyler.

"You've got good taste, young man," the jeweler said. "Natural emeralds that color are hard to find. Rare."

"How much?" Tyler handed the ring to J.T. for him to get a closer look at it.

The jeweler took out his calculator, typed in some numbers. "After the family discount? With tax, fifty-two hundred."

"That's the one?" Tyler asked J.T. while he reached for his wallet.

J.T. handed the ring back to the jeweler with a nod.

"Wrap it up." Tyler handed his credit card over.

The ring came back wrapped in pretty red paper with a fancy bow. After Tyler signed the receipt, they left the store. Back in the truck, J.T. put his seat belt on, but this time he didn't immediately put his earbuds in his ears and turn on his music.

"If you married my mom, where would I live?"

Tyler turned on the truck and shifted into gear. "At the ranch with us."

"I know…" J.T. gave a little teenager sigh as if it were

impossible to communicate with adults. "But *where*? Your cabin only has two bedrooms."

The fact that the boy was even asking this question was major progress, and Tyler knew it. He just tried to not show it too much on the outside.

More casually than he felt on the inside, Tyler said, "I'll show you where you can stay when we get home. How's that?"

## Chapter Fourteen

Back at the ranch, London spread out all of the new baby clothes on the bed and admired them. She picked up each tiny, frilly, totally girlie item one by one. If her daughter turned out to be a tomboy like her, at least she could dress her like a girl for a while before she started to reject dresses for jeans. London was still admiring her purchases when she heard a thump directly above her head.

"Tyler? J.T.?"

When neither responded, she put the little ruffled purple top down and went in search of her son and her cowboy. More thumps that sounded like footsteps overhead made her stop and look upward.

"Hey! Where are you guys?"

"We're upstairs." She heard Tyler's voice, but she

didn't know where upstairs was in the cabin. In fact, she didn't even know that an upstairs existed.

She followed their voices down the hall, past the guest bedroom and found an open door at the end of the hall. She peered into what she had always believed to be a linen closet, only to discover a set of drop-down wooden attic stairs.

"Come up." Tyler stood at the top of the landing and held out his hand to her.

She carefully climbed the steps. At the top, she took his hand and he held on to her until she could safely stand on her own two feet.

"I didn't even know this was here!" London put her hands on her hips and looked around at the attic space. Tyler had already insulated and drywalled and installed hand-scraped wooden floors that appeared to be re-claimed wood.

J.T. was exploring the large space that ran the length of the cabin very intently.

"What are you guys doing up here?"

"Just checking it out," Tyler said nonchalantly.

"It's a beautiful space." London walked over to a large picture window that looked out to the mountains. She had never had a reason to walk behind the house and had never noticed the window at the peak of the cabin.

"What are you planning to do with it?"

"I was going to put a pool table up here," Tyler explained. "Have my own bar over there. Just a place to hang out with the boys during the winter."

London's brows dropped at the thought. "Not very practical to have a bar in a house with a baby."

"You're right about that," he agreed.

J.T. came over to where they were standing.

"What do you think?" Tyler asked her son.

J.T. nodded a little, which was about as expressive as he got these days. "It's pretty sweet up here."

"Could you live with it?"

"I'm sorry?" London looked between them. "What am I missing? Can he live with what?"

"This…as a bedroom," Tyler said.

"A bedroom." London restated it. "A *bedroom*?"

"Sure." Tyler was serious. "Why not? We have the master. We can turn the guest room into the nursery. We need a third bedroom."

"And another bathroom," J.T. added.

"And a third bathroom." Tyler agreed with him.

"It's *huge* up here…a kid doesn't need this much space."

Tyler kept on talking as if he hadn't heard her.

"Over here…we could make this your chilling-out area…get a flat screen, hook up some video games." Tyler was getting more excited about the buildout as he designed the space. "What do you think?"

He was asking J.T., not her. This was a strange, annoying scene. It was nice that Tyler was thinking of a space for her son, but this was too much. She had to fight his father with the spoiling…she didn't want to have to fight Tyler, too.

"We tap into the plumbing for the guest bathroom right here…" J.T. was standing with Tyler now instead of her. "And you still have plenty of space for a king-size bed and a desk."

"It sounded like elephants walking around up here when I was downstairs…"

"We'll soundproof." Tyler wasn't deterred.

J.T. looked at Tyler, then looked at her. "I could live with this."

"Oh…" She laughed. "I know you could! What kid wouldn't want his own apartment before he turns thirteen?"

Tyler went down the ladder first and waited at the bottom for her to climb down safely. She could see that Tyler's idea for an upstairs apartment had really grabbed J.T.'s attention.

When Tyler left to get some work done before the sun began to set and the temperature dropped to below freezing, London knocked on the guest bedroom door. J.T. was lying down on the bed, listening to his music too loud. She sat down on the edge of the bed and patted him on the leg.

"Hey…do you think you could unplug for two seconds and actually talk to me?"

J.T. pushed himself up and back against the pillows, pulled his earbuds out of his ears.

"What's up?"

London shook her head. "No. Not polite, J.T. Turn the music *off* and talk to me."

J.T. turned off the music with a dramatic sigh.

"I'm over here…"

"What?" This was said in that whiny tone she disliked so much. When would he outgrow that one?

"Look…I *know* you're mad at me, okay? I get it. And you have a right to be mad at me." She started counting on her fingers. "I broke my promise to you, I hid things from you—which is too close to a lie *not* to be a lie—I'm pregnant, and I want you to leave your life and all of your friends in Virginia to move to a really ridiculously cold ranch in Montana."

J.T. stared hard at her with his father's dark brown eyes.

"I let you down," London admitted. "And I'm sorry."

Her son looked away from her and she saw him start to tear up.

"I'm sorry, J.T." She put her hand on his arm. "I really am. But shutting me out, not talking to me, isn't going to make things better. I promise you that. I've tried it with my parents already, and look where that got me with them, right? Grandpa has all but disowned me at this point, and Gram is perpetually disappointed with my choices…"

She turned her body toward him. "I hate that I've disappointed you. I do. But I can't change it. All I can do is try to make this work for the three of us…you, me and this baby."

"Tyler told me that he wants to marry you."

London knew the surprise showed on her face. "He asked. And I told him I couldn't marry him if you weren't going to be happy here at the ranch." She looked directly into her son's eyes so he knew she was dead serious. "I mean it, J.T. If you can't be happy in Montana, then I won't marry Tyler. If you're not happy, I can't be happy."

London saw a mixture of anger and doubt in her son's eyes. "So…what? You'll just go back to Virginia?"

"If you're not going to be happy here, J.T., then I won't be happy. If that means we leave Montana…then we leave Montana. You, me…" She put her hand on her stomach. "And Maggie."

"What's wrong with it?"

Tyler had been so focused on the sickly calf that

he hadn't heard J.T. approach. He straightened with a heavy sigh.

"She's sick. Been sick from day one. I can't seem to get her to eat."

J.T. hung over the gate. "Where's her mom?"

"She died." Tyler didn't feel the need to hide the truth from J.T. He was a solid kid.

"It never fails," Tyler continued with a frustrated shake of his head. "It snows and all the cows want to give birth. Why on the coldest nights, I'll never know."

"Can I come in there?"

"Sure." Tyler swung the gate open. "She'll like the company. Gotta be scary as all get-out to find yourself in a brand-new world without a mom to protect you."

J.T. sat down in the deep bed of hay Tyler had created for the calf.

"She's so soft," the boy noted. "Why aren't you eating?"

"I think it's the consistency... I don't have it close enough to her mother's milk. Or," Tyler added, "maybe it's the nipple on the bottle. I've tried all of my normal tricks. But none of it's working with this one."

J.T. kept his hand on the calf's neck. "What's her name?"

"I haven't named her."

"Maybe she needs a name."

"If she doesn't have the will to live, a name isn't going to make the difference." Tyler's frustration came through in his tone and in the words he chose. He didn't like to be helpless and sometimes with nature, no matter how hard he tried, he *was* helpless.

Tyler paused at the stall door. J.T. was gently petting the calf.

"Hey…if you want to name her—" Tyler tapped the wood with his fingers "—go ahead."

Tyler was out of the stall when J.T. called him back inside.

"Mom seems really happy when she's with you," J.T. said.

Tyler tried to keep his expression neutral. This was the conversation he had been waiting to have with London's son ever since the jewelry store. He had to wait for J.T. to come to him. The ball was in his court now.

"She hasn't always been that happy, you know." J.T. rubbed the top of the calf's head. "She never used to smile all that much."

Tyler gave J.T. plenty of time to continue. The kid was on a roll and he didn't want to stop him now.

"So…if you want to marry my mom." The teenager finally looked up at him. "I suppose it's okay with me."

Tyler didn't move for a second or two. He didn't even think that he blinked at first. He had no idea how stressful it had been to have the control of his future, his *daughter's* future, placed in J.T.'s young hands, until it was over.

"Thank you," Tyler finally said with a catch in his throat.

J.T. didn't seem to hear him. Or maybe he didn't know what to say. He didn't respond to his thank-you, but did ask, "Can I try to feed her?"

The question was unexpected. But he got it. He wasn't big on emotional conversations, either. "Sure. Maybe you'll succeed where I've failed."

That night, in the dark, Tyler held London's hand and stared up at the ceiling he had stared at hundreds of times before. But tonight was different. He was holding the hand of his future wife. When he built this cabin, he had imagined his perfect bachelor pad. He hadn't thought about a future wife or a stepson or a daughter. Yet that's what had unfolded. God's plan was much better, much grander, than the simple plan he'd had for himself.

"I'm sorry I don't feel like making love." London broke the silence.

"Don't worry about it." He smiled in the dark and squeezed her fingers to reassure her. "There's more to our relationship than sex."

London turned to face him, curled her body into his. Her stomach, rounder and heavier, pressed into his side.

"I've never seen your parents argue before," she said. "I didn't know what to do. I wanted to hide under the table, to tell you the truth. Really uncomfortable."

"Dad's not really loving the new heart-healthy diet… He's always been a red-meat man," Tyler said. "But they'll work it out. Dad eventually gives in, Mom wins…that's how it's worked for nearly fifty years."

"Fifty years… I can't even imagine that."

"I can." Tyler didn't hesitate for a moment. Like his parents and his grandparents before, he planned on marrying only once.

Christmas Eve at the Brand family farmhouse was a dressy affair. The elastic of her one black skirt was stretched to the limit by her belly and the matching blouse wouldn't button over her breasts. With a stressed-out, frustrated sound, she pulled the blouse off, balled it up and threw it on the floor.

"What's wrong?" Tyler came out of the bathroom,

freshly shaved, hair slicked back. He looked so handsome in his slacks and button-down shirt that she had to admire him.

"You look…really handsome, Tyler."

Tyler smiled at her. He leaned down and kissed her naked belly before he asked again, "What's wrong?"

"Nothing fits. I don't have anything to wear and Barb said that dinner was going to be served promptly at six!"

"Hey…relax. It's just another dinner."

"No, it's not. And I don't want to be late. Or topless."

"Why don't you try on one of the shirts Sophia gave you?"

London scrunched up her face. Sophia had found some of her old maternity tops up in the attic and had been sweet enough to wash them for her.

"I didn't think I needed a maternity top just yet." She frowned.

"What about this one?" Tyler had the closet open and pulled out one of the hand-me-down blouses.

The blouse wasn't bad, but it just wasn't her. It was too…feminine.

"You look pretty," Tyler told her.

"When did I get so huge?" She looked down at her protruding stomach as if she were really seeing it for the first time.

Tyler grabbed her hand. "Come on… Mom's sweet potato pie is calling my name."

Once she walked through the front door of the house, she forgot all about how uncomfortable she was in the hand-me-down maternity top and immersed herself in the smells and the sounds of the Brand family Christmas Eve. There was a large fire roaring to keep the house warm while the snow began to fall outside again.

The sweet-smelling Christmas tree was covered in twinkling lights and candy canes, and the kitchen was bustling with activity. Sophia and Luke's twin daughters were up from their nap, full of energy and keeping their parents on their toes. Little Danny was sitting on his grandfather's lap. And of course, Ilsa and Ranger were loitering near the stove, hoping for a handout.

"A lot different than our Christmas Eve," she said to her son, who seemed to be a little overwhelmed, too.

"There're presents under the tree for me," J.T. told her.

She hugged him quickly. "Are you surprised?"

He shrugged one shoulder, as if he could care less about the presents. "I wonder what Gram and Pop are doing."

"Pop is in his chair," she predicted. "And Gram is yelling at him because he never fixed the handle on the stove."

"I miss them," J.T. admitted.

"Yeah…" she agreed. "I miss them, too. We'll call them later."

At her mom's house, there was always yelling and grousing and something burning in the oven that had been on the blink for fifteen years. The Brand family holiday felt like a Norman Rockwell painting come to life, and she loved it. She had always wondered what it would be like to live in one of those paintings when she was a kid, and now here she was. Living the dream. And yet she still missed that tiny house in the lower-middle-class neighborhood where she grew up. No matter how well Barb and Sophia cooked, no one would ever be able to match her mom's stuffing.

They sat down promptly at six and London ended

up eating way more food than she needed to eat. Normally after dinner, the men would have whiskey and a cigar, but after Hank's heart attack, that tradition had to change. After the table was cleared and the dishes washed, the family moved to the family room. Abigail was asleep in her mother's arms, but Annabelle was wide-awake and fussing on Luke's lap.

"We've got to put them down," Luke said to his wife. "They don't know what's going on yet anyway."

"Okay…" Sophia let her husband take Abigail. "We'll wait for you."

When Luke returned, each person was able to open one present. It was tradition. One by one, presents were handed out and opened. But London didn't receive a present. She watched while the rest of the family ripped the paper off their presents and wondered why no one, including Tyler and her son, noticed that she didn't have a present.

"Mom…" J.T. was smiling enough to show his teeth. "Look."

J.T. had a brand-new gaming system in front of him.

"Tyler…" London shook her head. "That's too much."

"Don't look at me."

"Oh, I'm sorry, London." Sophia held a bottle of perfume in her hands. "That was me."

"Make sure you say thank-you, J.T.," London told him. She couldn't be mad at Sophia for being kind to her son, could she?

"Thanks, Sophia."

"I'm glad you like it."

"Can I hook it up to your TV?" J.T. asked Tyler.

"Heck yeah… I'll play it with you."

The family cleaned up their wrapping paper and Barb signaled that it was time to wind up the night.

"Wait a minute!" Barb said. "London didn't get a present!"

The entire family started to talk at once.

"Don't worry about it," London said. "More for me tomorrow."

"No…" Barb shook her head. "Absolutely not. J.T.— why don't you grab that box right there and give it to your mom."

J.T. got a small box from beneath the tree and handed it to her. She unwrapped it and then realized that it was a ring box.

Her heart started to palpitate and she started to perspire. This was a *ring* box. She felt the eyes of the family on her as she slowly cracked open the box. Inside was a lovely dark green emerald, surrounded by round bright white diamonds set in yellow gold.

She met Tyler's eyes. "It's the prettiest ring I've ever seen."

"May I?" Tyler took the ring out of the box.

He took her hand and held it as he went down on one knee. Her knees were shaking, and she couldn't look at anyone other than Tyler.

"London…" Tyler held the ring poised at the end of her left-hand ring finger. "In front of my family, in front of your son…I want you to know that I love you and I want you to be my wife. Will you do me the honor of marrying me?"

She couldn't seem to get even one word out of her mouth, so she nodded silently instead.

"Is that a yes?" Tyler smiled at her.

She looked over at J.T. When her son gave his nod of

approval, she felt free to finally say the words she had wanted to say to Tyler for months.

"Yes." She watched him slip the ring onto her finger. "I want to marry you, Tyler. I will marry you."

## Chapter Fifteen

"Merry Christmas…"

London heard the deep timbre of Tyler's familiar voice through the fog of sleep. She rolled over onto her back and tried to pry her eyes open. She hadn't slept well the night before; the baby had been moving and kicking. Her back was starting to ache all the time. And even though they didn't hurt, she had noticed in the bathtub that she now had cankles instead of ankles.

"Merry Christmas, Ell." Tyler's voice was stronger and clearer now. The fog was lifting.

London stretched, yawned, snuggled more deeply into the covers and then slowly blinked her eyes open.

"What are you wearing?" She had meant to say, "Merry Christmas," but when she got her first look at her fiancé, the question just popped right out of her mouth instead.

Tyler spun around for her and showed off his costume. "I'm Santa."

London shook her head a little in denial. "Did Santa go on a serious diet over the summer? Because Santa isn't skinny."

Tyler had on a head-to-toe Santa costume, with red hat and fake white beard included. He looked down at his flat belly.

"Good point. Hold that thought." Tyler left the room and then returned. He modeled left to right for her. "How about now?"

London propped herself up on one elbow. "Well…if stomachs come in *square*, then you're pulling off that look, I'd say."

Tyler patted the couch pillow stuffed into his costume. "Ho! Ho! Ho!"

"A little deeper," she instructed. "Santa's voice is deeper."

Tyler sat down next to her on the bed and said in a deeper voice, "Want to give Santa a kiss, little girl?"

Tyler started to kiss her ear, which was her most ticklish spot, with his tickly synthetic beard and his breath. She started to squirm and squeal.

"Quit it! You're freaking me out!" She pushed on his shoulder and fake pillow stomach, laughing and trying to escape Santa's clutches.

"Give me a kiss and I'll let you go…" Tyler had her trapped between his two arms.

London scrunched up her face and gave him a quick kiss. You were *not* supposed to kiss Santa! There was something inherently wrong with that act.

"Merry Christmas." Tyler laughed.

"Merry Christmas." London was up and out of bed. "Why are you torturing me?"

Tyler stood up and readjusted his pillow. "Mom told me to come get you up, so that's what I'm doing. Everyone's at the house and we're ready to open presents."

"J.T.?"

"At the house…already had breakfast." Tyler opened the curtains and let the light flood into the room.

London looked at the window. "It's snowing! It's snowing on Christmas!"

"Yes. It's snowing on Christmas. Pretty much every year." Tyler wasn't impressed. "Hurry up, poky! Mom's about to have a conniption fit. Now, if you'll excuse me, I have children to delight."

It was hard to believe that she had actually slept in late on Christmas morning. That had never happened before. She had always been mother and father on Christmas, so she had to stay up after J.T. had gone to bed to put the presents under the tree, get some last-minute wrapping done and put together toys that needed to be assembled. Sometimes her stepfather would help her if his health would allow, but her mother never really enjoyed Christmas and usually went to bed early.

She quickly dressed, wrapped up in her winter gear and then made the short trek in the freshly fallen snow to the main house. When she walked into the kitchen, she was greeted by all of the Brand voices.

"Merry Christmas!"

She had never received so many hugs on Christmas morning. Everyone hugged her, but the hug that meant the most was the hard, genuine Christmas hug she received from her son. He looked rested, well fed and happy. Her concerns that J.T. wouldn't feel comfortable with the Brands had been unfounded. He fit in with the family as if he had always belonged to them. His face told the story—he felt accepted here…and happy.

London kissed her son on his warm cheek. "Merry Christmas, son."

"Merry Christmas, Mom."

Barb made her a plate for breakfast and she sat down at the table with Hank, Luke and Sophia. After she finished, everyone piled into the family room. The presents under the tree had multiplied overnight and Tyler, in his costume, was waiting by the tree to hand out presents.

"Ho! Ho! Ho!" Tyler bellowed. "Merry Christmas!"

Annabelle took one look at Tyler in his Santa costume and started to scream at the top of her lungs. Luke scooped her up, turned around so she couldn't see Tyler and started to bounce her to distract her. Abigail walked over to Tyler on her chubby, unsteady legs and grabbed on to the red velvet pant leg of his costume.

Tyler picked up his niece and looked at her carefully. "Have you been naughty or nice, Abigail?"

Sophia and Luke exchanged knowing looks. Their girls had successfully entered the terrible twos. In unison, they both said, "Naughty."

"Have you been naughty?" Tyler asked Abigail. Abigail shook her head no and pulled on his beard.

Tyler passed out the presents one by one. There were so many gifts beneath the tree for her that it looked as if she was building a fort out of presents. Barb had bought everything baby that she could think of and she was set for at least a year in supplies and baby clothing. J.T. had been spoiled with a stack of video games for his gaming system, as well as clothing. The tree had nearly been emptied of presents when Tyler came across a small hastily wrapped box.

"Here's one for J.T." Tyler handed London's son the box.

"Don't get mad…it was Dad's idea," Tyler whispered to her.

London watched her son unwrap the present. What in the world had Hank bought her son now? She felt that the Brands had already gone above and beyond what needed to be done in order to give her son an amazing first Christmas at Bent Tree Ranch. What else could he possibly want?

J.T. took a key out of the box and held it up. "What's this go to?"

"I suppose we'll all have to go out to the barn to find out," Hank said with a little twinkle in his deeply set blue eyes.

London reached out and held on to Santa's sleeve. "*What* did you buy him?"

Tyler held out his hand so he could help her up. "I didn't buy it for him…Dad did," Tyler assured her. "Just don't freak out."

They all bundled up and headed out the barn. London spotted the gift at the same time her son let out a loud shout of surprise and joy. J.T. sprinted the last couple of yards to the present.

London was in shock. Her son was sitting on a brand-new bright red snowmobile with a giant white bow stuck on the headlight.

"I can't believe it!" J.T.'s voice had gone up an octave. "This is mine? Are you serious?"

Hank was grinning. "She's all yours."

London wanted to protest. She wanted to order her

son off the snowmobile with a list of reason why it wasn't safe. She wanted to tell Hank that she hoped he'd saved his receipt because he needed to pack it up and take it back to the store. She wanted to be furious that Tyler had obviously known what Hank had in mind for a present and he hadn't told her. And she wanted to be indignant that Hank had bought this kind of present for her son without even asking her. She wanted to be a lot of things. But the look on her son's face…the sheer joy in his eyes…she couldn't bring herself to do or say any of those things.

"Mom!" J.T. shouted at her with a wave.

She walked over to her ecstatic son. "This is quite a gift."

"It's the best Christmas gift I've ever gotten!" J.T. said with amazement.

"You'd better say thank-you to Hank and Barb," she told him.

Instead of just saying thank-you like she expected, J.T. got off the snowmobile and threw his arms around Hank's tall, lanky frame.

That was the moment. That was it. Standing outside on a snowy day, her breath forming willowy white curls in the air, the cold skin of her face wet with fresh flakes of snow, she saw her son embrace the Brand family. Yes, he embraced Hank with that hug. But she knew her son and now she was certain, beyond any reasonable doubt, that J.T. could, *would* be happy at Bent Tree Ranch. So, despite all of her reservations regarding the snowmobile…she couldn't take it away from him. The shiny red snowmobile with the big white bow and *J.T.* written on the card had to stay.

After the snowmobile reveal, everyone hurried back

to the house to get warmed up and clean up the wrapping paper and box mess in the family room. Tyler retired his Santa costume until next Christmas and when he returned from the cabin, he found London sitting in front of the fire. He sat down next to her, his arm resting on the back of the couch.

"How's your first Christmas at Bent Tree?"

She sent him a soft smile, her eyes full of love and gratitude. "What you did…what your family did for my son is…"

She didn't have the words. She simply did not have the words.

"We all—Mom, Dad, Luke, Sophia—we all wanted J.T. to feel like he was at home here." Tyler took her hand in his. "We did this for you. This is how we show our love for you."

"Thank you." She squeezed his fingers. "Seeing J.T. so happy makes me happy."

Tyler rubbed his finger over the stone of her engagement ring. "Seeing you happy makes me happy."

She put her hand on his cheek and then kissed him lightly on the lips. "I love you, Tyler."

"I love you." He pulled her closer into his body. "I want to go into town tomorrow and apply for a marriage license."

"Okay."

"I want to get married, in the chapel, before J.T. leaves for Virginia."

London spun her head around and looked up into his face. "That only gives us less than three weeks!"

"I know." Tyler nodded. "So we've got a lot of work to do."

"But…Barb and Sophia are already planning for

Danny's birthday party. We don't want our wedding to interfere with his birthday."

"It won't." He got up to stoke the fire.

"And who will perform the ceremony? Will we be able to get someone on such short notice?"

"Dad can marry us."

"Hank's a justice of the peace?"

Tyler nodded, sat back down. "He doesn't like to do it, but we may be able to talk him into it."

"And I don't have anything to wear," she worried out loud. She hadn't even considered getting married *before* she gave birth.

"Look…" Tyler cut her off. "Do you want to be my wife or not?"

"Yes."

"Then let's just strike while the iron's hot. J.T. picked out that ring you're wearing. He's given us his blessing. If we get this done before he leaves, he can be the one to walk you down the aisle."

Tyler was right. Walking her down the aisle was something that J.T. would like to do. He was that kind of kid. It would be meaningful to him.

"Okay," London agreed. "What day do you want to get married?"

Tyler took out a little black appointment book he always carried in his front pocket. He turned to January.

"How about two weeks from today?" he asked.

"Two weeks from today?" She smiled at him.

"Two weeks from today."

She teased him by pretending she had to think about it. Then she hooked her arm through his with a nod. "All right, cowboy. Let's get married."

\* \* \*

"How's it going in there, London?" Barbara Brand asked.

"Do you need some help?" Sophia's voice was the second she heard.

How was it going? Did she need some help?

London had known that wedding-dress shopping was going to be a challenge this far along in her pregnancy. It was *not* going well and she did need help, but the kind of help she needed had to come directly from the divine.

"I'll be out in just a minute…" London called out to her soon-to-be mother-in-law and sister-in-law.

To Sarah the wedding dress specialist, she asked, "Can you actually get this one zipped?"

They had been in the dressing room for at least thirty minutes and hadn't shown Barb or Sophia one dress. There were several she couldn't get over her head because she couldn't squeeze them over her breasts. There were several that she couldn't get up over her hips. She actually got into one dress that she loved and then realized that she looked like a giant sausage stuffed unflatteringly into ruched satin. And like just about everything she tried on, the length was too short for her height, six feet in bare feet. The very last option, and her least favorite by far, was an off-white chiffon gown with an empire waist, ruched bodice and spaghetti straps.

"It's zipped!" Sarah said with just a little bit too much enthusiasm. The bar for success in the appointment had been lowered way down—if something zipped up, it got a cheer.

London turned around to look in the full-length mirror. The top of the dress was too small for her overinflated pregnancy breasts and the flowing chiffon resembled a tent.

"And it's long enough," Sarah commented cheerfully. "Let's show them."

Sarah opened the curtain and revealed London as if she were introducing the Princess of Wales. London had to give it to the clerk…she had a flair for the dramatic, even under the worst of circumstances.

London stepped up onto the pedestal surrounded by three-way mirrors. Now that she could see herself multiplied times three, she knew that her only real dress option was *not* an option.

"There are way too many of me right now." London ran her hand over the flowing chiffon.

"I don't believe that's going to work." Barbara was a Chicago woman and highly fashionable… She saw exactly what London saw in the mirror.

"Let's not dismiss it too quickly, Mom." Sweet Sophia stood up and walked over to where she was standing.

"No…I agree with Barb…this isn't going to work."

"What don't you like about it?" Sophia asked. "That way we know what to avoid when we look for more dresses."

"Everything."

"No…really," Sophia pressed her. "What don't you like about it?"

"Besides everything?" London asked facetiously. "I hate the top part… I never wear strapless and I look like I have one gigantic boob up here. This chiffon reminds me of my mom's wedding dress from the '70s and it makes me look like the Goodyear blimp came to town early…"

"That's not nice to say." Sophia shook her head with a frown.

"The only thing nice I have to say about this entire getup is that it's long enough," she said to Sarah, who had been fluffing the skirt of the gown and trying to present the dress in its best light. "Can you get me out of this now?"

She came out of the dressing room in her own clothing.

"Are you done trying on for the day?" Barb asked her.

"I think I'm done for forever," London told her. "I'm too tall and too pregnant and it's too short notice to get a wedding dress."

"Then what are you going to wear?" Sophia was the most disappointed.

"I don't know." London put on her winter coat. "I just want to feel like myself when I marry Tyler."

"And what does feeling like yourself entail?" Barb asked.

It was a good question. "Jeans. Boots. A man's button-down."

"We could work with that theme." Barb's wheels were already turning. "This is the first wedding now that the inside of the chapel has been refurbished. Why not make it casual country chic?"

"I like the sound of that. Country chic." London felt like smiling for the first time that morning.

"We can dress it up a little with some accessories," Sophia added. "It will be perfect."

London climbed into the front seat of Barb's Range Rover, glad to be heading back to the ranch. She buckled her seat belt then turned to look at Sophia in the backseat.

"Any day that I get to marry Tyler will be a perfect day."

"Aw…" Sophia instinctively reached forward to squeeze her arm. "You're such a sweetheart."

On the drive home, the three of them used the time to make plans for a quick, casual country-chic wedding. Barb had a lot of friends who would be willing to pitch in to get the wedding organized quickly. They already had the venue, and now that London had decided that jeans and boots were going to be the dress code, outfits weren't going to be a concern.

"You know, London," Barb said. "I've seen a big change in Tyler since you've been in his life."

"I have, too," Sophia agreed.

"Really?" London looked at both Barb and Sophia in turn.

"He's turned into a genuine grown-up, don't you think?" Sophia laughed. "I personally thought that we had another George Clooney on our hands. A bachelor until he was in his fifties."

"I certainly didn't have any hopes of grandchildren from Tyler in this decade," Barb told London. "And the fact that he's so excited about being a father… I didn't expect that from Tyler. I honestly thought if he ever did settle down that he'd be much more hands-off."

"He's wanted to go to every appointment…be a part of everything," London agreed. "I've been completely surprised by him. He's got that cowboy swagger going on…"

"Honestly," Sophia added. "I've only ever seen him get this excited over livestock, horseflesh and Ranger. You've brought out a whole different side of Tyler that none of us have ever seen."

## Chapter Sixteen

London looked at her reflection in the mirror and she actually liked what she saw. She was wearing comfortable jeans that had an elastic band built in to accommodate her belly. Sophia had helped her find a pretty white cotton top with long sleeves and just enough feminine touches to make her feel like a bride. She wore her hair down, straight and long, because Tyler loved it that way.

She turned away from her reflection when she heard a knock at the door. "Come in."

J.T. opened the door and poked his head inside.

"Hey…where have you been?" she asked.

He came into the bedroom. "I had to feed Jasmine." Her son sat down on the bed. "Tyler said that she's mine, so she'll still be at the ranch when I get back."

"What are you going to do with a full-grown cow, J.T.?"

"I don't know," her son said. "But she's not going to end up on someone's plate."

London turned to give her son a look. "Was it necessary to go there?"

"I'm just saying…"

London fidgeted with her top a little more. "Okay… how do I look?"

J.T. examined her seriously. "You look pretty."

"Do I look like a bride?"

Her son thought some more. "I'm not sure. But pretty."

"All right," she said. "I'll take pretty. Did you talk to your father?"

J.T. nodded with a frown. "He sounded mad. I thought he'd be happy for you or something…"

London hugged her son. She leaned back but kept her hands on his shoulders. "That's adult stuff. That's not for you to worry about. Okay?"

"Okay…" He nodded. "I wish Gram and Pop were going to be here."

Her mom couldn't get off work, but she didn't like to fly anyway, and her stepfather wouldn't come without her. Her biological father wasn't interested in her wedding plans, so she hadn't invited him to the wedding. He would just find a way to sour the day, and that was the sad truth. She didn't have a whole lot of family, but after today she would have the Brand family to call her own.

"I'm going to head up to the chapel now," her son told her.

"Well, wait a minute." She waved her hand. "Don't I even get a hug?"

Her son let her hug him and he hugged her back. After the hug, they held hands, face-to-face.

"Ever since the first day I found out I was pregnant with you, we were in this thing together. Do you know that? You and me. We're a team. No matter what. And today we're going to join the Brand family...together. It doesn't work unless you're with me. You got that?"

J.T. nodded and gave her a little smile. It was enough.

Then she was alone again. Everyone would be up at the chapel now. Tyler's sisters, Jordan and Josephine, were upset that they couldn't get home on such short notice. But they understood that having J.T. walk her down the aisle before he went back to Virginia was more important.

A knock on the door sent her heart racing. This was it. Today she would become a bride... Tyler Brand's bride.

"Are you ready?" Hank Brand opened the front door of the cabin.

She nodded and followed him out to the horse-drawn buggy. Hank looked dapper in his dark-washed jeans, white shirt, black hat and black jacket. He helped her into the buggy and they took off up the hill for the chapel. The ride was a bit bumpy with all the divots dug into the dirt road by the melting and refreezing of the snow. It wasn't the most romantic thought to have as she approached the chapel, but she hoped—prayed— that her bladder would hold throughout the ceremony. The chapel didn't have a place for a pit stop and the baby seemed to be parked right on top of her bladder.

J.T. was waiting for her outside the chapel. He helped her down out of the buggy. Hank parked the horses so he could take his seat inside. Hank had refused to marry them, no matter how many times or ways Tyler tried to get him to agree. It turned out that the one couple Hank had married was divorced now and he didn't want to jinx the whole deal. Luckily, the priest who had married Tyler's sister Jordan and her husband, Ian, made himself available to the family.

Once Hank had taken his place at the front of the chapel next to his wife, J.T. offered her his arm and they walked up the old stone steps together. Luke closed the doors behind them to keep the frigid winter air out. It was still cold in the chapel—she noticed that right away. The chapel was more than one hundred years old and didn't have modern amenities. Previous work on the chapel had required power, so at least the family had been able to bring in some space heaters to cut the harsh chill. But it was still cold. She could see her breath as she walked down the aisle toward Tyler with her son.

There wasn't any music. Only silence. It seemed more reverent, perhaps even a little more special, without the music. The only thing she really heard was the sound of her own heartbeat pounding in her ears. She was staring at Tyler, her cowboy...the man who would be her husband and the father of her first daughter. He was so handsome. So *handsome* to her eyes. He was tall and lanky like his father, with sandy hair from his mother's side and those incredible bright blue Brand eyes. He was, quite simply, the perfect man for her. A match.

"Who gives this woman to this man?" the priest asked when they reached the end of the short aisle.

"I do," J.T. said. He seemed so grown to her. It had happened so fast...right under her nose.

"We do, too!" The few family members who were able to attend the wedding had to add their two cents to the ceremony. And why not? She had wanted a casual, country-chic wedding, after all.

Tyler held out his hand to her. She kissed her son on the cheek before she took the last couple of steps to Tyler on her own.

Hand in hand, they faced each other. They stared intently into each other's eyes, unafraid of what they saw inside the other while the priest walked them through their vows. One at a time, they slipped simple gold bands on to their ring fingers. And then at last, at long last, the priest said the words they had both been waiting to hear.

"I am happy to pronounce Tyler Brand and London Davenport Brand husband and wife. Tyler...you may now kiss your bride."

Right there in front of God, his family and her son, Tyler grabbed her, dipped her and then kissed her on the lips. When he brought her back up, he had a trace of Mostly Mauve lipstick on his lips. The family cheered for them, and with a happy laugh, London wiped the lipstick off her husband's lips.

"Can we get the heck out of here now?" she asked Tyler. "I'm freezing my pregnant butt off!"

After the ceremony, they all returned to the main house to celebrate. Barb had baked her famous three-layer chocolate cake, Tyler's favorite, for the wedding and she'd promised to let Hank cheat on his diet just for the day.

"I am so sorry the twins started to cry during the ceremony." Sophia approached her. "I really thought about getting someone to watch them."

"It wouldn't have been the same without them." London shook her head.

In fact, the ceremony, the wedding, had been perfect. The chapel was old and drafty, the twins had cried, and

Danny playing with his trains on the floor so close to the podium had distracted the priest from his routine. The priest had kept on talking louder and louder to drown out the sound of the little plastic wheels running over uneven wooden floors. At one point, the priest was nearly shouting at them. And halfway through the ceremony, her fear became reality and her bladder started to hurt. By the time they got the kiss, she felt as though her bladder was going to burst. But it was their wedding. It was their day. So it was perfect.

Her mother-in-law took her plate after she had devoured a second piece of chocolate cake and put an envelope in its place.

"What's this?"

"Open it…" Barb had an excited expression on her face. She was definitely up to something.

London didn't pick the envelope up. "But you've already done so much for us already."

Earlier Hank and Barb had given them a check big enough to cover the renovations to create a third bedroom in the cabin for her son. It was a very large check. In fact, she'd never actually seen a check that big in person before.

"This is from me to you…mother to daughter." Barb had that *I'm not taking no for an answer* kind of look on her face. "Open it!"

London picked up the envelope and pulled the flap open. Inside was a thin piece of paper. She unfolded it, and when she saw what it was, she couldn't stop herself. She started to cry.

"What is it?" Tyler took the paper out of London's hands.

"She gave me Rising Sun." London's voice was wobbly with emotion. She stood up, went to Barb and flung her arms around her neck.

"Welcome to the family, London." Barb hugged her new daughter-in-law tightly. "I think he's always belonged to you."

"I give her a ring and marry her and I didn't get tears," he said to his father. "Mom gives her a horse and waterworks?"

"It doesn't make a bit of sense, son, but you may as well start getting used to it," Hank told him.

London wiped the tears off her face, blew her now red nose and rejoined her husband.

"Well...I don't know how I'm going to follow that female bonding moment, but I do have something special planned for tonight," Tyler said.

"What?" She had thought that they would be spending their first night as a married couple in the cabin.

"You'll see."

But she didn't see. Not at first. Because she *couldn't* see. He blindfolded her, which she didn't like, and put her in the truck. No matter how many times she asked for a hint, he wouldn't budge.

"Okay..." She heard Tyler shift into Park and shut off the engine. "Take off your blindfold."

She pulled the blindfold off and looked through the windshield.

"Oh! It's beautiful."

Tyler had brought her to the tree house where they had first found out that she was pregnant with their daughter. A large "Happy Honeymoon" sign hung on the trees and the family had decorated the stairs that led up to the tree house.

"Let's go inside and get you warm."

Tyler met her on her side of the truck, offered her his hand, and they walked, holding hands, through the thin layer of snow and ice to the tree house. The stairs had been cleared of ice, which made it safe for her to navigate now that she was in her third trimester.

Tyler held the door open for her and she walked into the magical house way up high in the trees. Someone had already been there—a fire was built, and there was a plate of chocolate-covered strawberries and sparkling grape juice on the table.

"Who did all of this?"

"Luke and Sophia." Tyler helped her out of her coat. "They wanted to do something special for us."

London looked around at the thoughtful touches that had Sophia's hand. She had created a large mobile of pictures of her and Tyler and J.T. on the ranch.

"Your family is unreal." London sat down on the love seat in wonder. "I didn't even know that people like your parents, your brother, your sisters even existed."

"Brands take care of their own." Tyler hung up his winter coat and hat. "Now you're a Brand and J.T.'s a Brand. I'll take care of him, London."

She put her hand on his cheek. "I know you will."

"And I'll take care of you…" He put his hand on her stomach. "And our little girl."

She kissed him lightly on the lips. "And I will take care of you, Tyler Brand. For the rest of my life… I promise that I will always be by your side."

They ate a couple of the strawberries and drank a little bit of the sparkling grape juice, but they were both full from the festivities earlier. Tyler made a makeshift bed in front of the fire and they both took off some of their clothes to get more comfortable.

London looked down at her maximum-coverage hold-'em-in-place support bra and matching pregnancy panties.

"I wish I could have worn some sexy lingerie for our wedding night." She frowned down at her body.

Tyler, who had stripped off his shirt and his socks, walked over to her, bare chested and barefoot. Without a comment, he took her into his arms and kissed her. There was so much packed into that kiss: love, desire, tenderness and friendship.

"Are you tired?" He brushed a strand of hair away from her face.

"I really am," she admitted. It had already been a long day.

"Let's lie down in front of the fire…if you fall asleep, you fall asleep."

"That isn't much of a honeymoon night for you."

"Hey," he told her sincerely. "You're here with me. That's all that matters. Okay?"

And so she slept in his arms in front of the fire, high up in the mountains of Montana. Tyler slept, too. When she awakened, he had flipped onto his stomach and he was sound asleep. She didn't want to wake him, so she went to the bathroom with the superdeep claw-foot tub and drew a bath.

She twisted her hair up on top of her head to keep it from getting wet. Sophia…thoughtful Sophia had left sweet-smelling bath beads next to the bathtub for her. She felt as though she was in heaven, sinking into the steaming water with the tree canopy, heavy with icy white snow, as her view. After her bath, she wrapped up in a towel and went back to her husband.

He was on his back now, still fast asleep. She lay

down facing him so she could watch him sleep. Lately, she hadn't been feeling sexy. Lately, she had been feeling *round*. Tyler didn't approach her as much for intimacy now... He had been giving her space. It was very possible that he wouldn't even try to make love to her tonight.

*That's not going to work.*

London had to make her first decision as Tyler's wife. They were going to make love tonight. She let the towel fall away from her body. The fire heated the skin of her naked back as she ran her hand over his chest, over his flat abdomen and down to the snap of his jeans. Tyler stirred but didn't open his eyes when she unsnapped and unzipped his jeans. He did, however, open his eyes and look at her when she slipped her hands into his underwear.

"Hi..." she said with an impish smile.

"Hi..." he said groggily. He glanced down at his groin. "Can I help you?"

"As a matter a fact, Mr. Brand..." London tightened her grip on his shaft. "You can."

He eyed her heavy breasts hungrily, but his next question was one of concern. "How are you feeling?"

"Like I want to make love to my husband."

Tyler smiled that sensual smile he reserved only for her. He stripped out of his jeans and stood before her naked, half-erect, looking like the most beautiful man she'd ever seen. She moved up onto her knees, so she could take him into her mouth. He hadn't expected it, so his gasp of surprise and pleasure was exactly what she wanted. She wrapped her tongue around the salty tip of his cock, drawing him deeper into the hot cavern of her mouth. He was hard and thick and ready to please her now. She kissed the inside of his thigh and then looked up at him. He was looking down at her, watching her pleasure him, with the look of a man who lusted after his own wife.

He took her hand and helped her to her feet. Together, they climbed the spiral staircase up to the second-story bedroom. It was there that he loved her as his wife for the first time. The contrast between the coolness of the air and the heat of his skin—everything was pleasure.

Tyler's hands knew her body. His mouth knew her body. Before he entered her, he always wanted to have the taste of her first orgasm on his lips—on his tongue. And when she could get herself into the mood, everything down *there* was so incredibly sensitive.

His tongue just kept working and working and the sensations got stronger and stronger until she felt herself wanting to...

"Ah!" She pushed down on his head and lifted up her hips. "Tyler!"

He devoured her with his mouth until she rode the last waves of an orgasm like none other. Her entire body had been jolted by it.

Tyler was laughing as he lay down next to her on his back.

"How was that for you?"

"Holy moly!" London laughed. "I didn't even know that my body could do that!"

She turned toward him, wrapped her fingers around his shaft to keep him hard.

"I have no idea what position is going to work, Tyler...we're just going to have to experiment a little..."

"I can do that."

On top, her hips hurt too much. With him on top,

she felt as if she couldn't breathe. Doggy style, he was too long and went in too deep.

"I'm running out of ideas," Tyler said.

They had both been chuckling through their third-trimester sex foibles. Her belly was in the way! Every time they failed at another position, Tyler's arousal level waned.

"We are going to make love, Tyler! It's our first night as a married couple!" London was determined to make this work.

She lay down on her side. "We haven't tried this one."

Tyler pressed his chest into her back and they curled their bodies into a C.

"You haven't lost it, have you?"

"Shh," he whispered against her neck. "Don't talk."

She closed her eyes and tried to relax. If it didn't happen, then, okay, it didn't happen. Tyler had one hand supporting her heavy belly, while the other arm was under her body so he could massage her breast. He moved behind her, slowly, slowly, kissing her neck, arousing her nipple. And then he slipped his long shaft inside her.

"Oh…" Her head fell back.

He groaned her name into her neck. Connected now, they intertwined their legs and threaded their fingers together. This was love. This was an abiding love.

"You are the love of my life, Ell…" It was a lover's confession.

Slow and sensual, Tyler stroked the inside of her body, driving her higher and higher until she shuddered with another orgasm. Her orgasm was the prize he had been seeking. He quickened his pace, holding on to her shoulders to drive her body downward onto his shaft.

"Ah!" Tyler surged forward one last time before he exploded inside her.

After his release, Tyler curled back around her and they held each other while the snow started to fall outside. He turned her in his arms so he was on his back and she had her head on his shoulder.

"Do you know how much I love you, London?" her husband asked. "Do you have any idea how much?"

Every day, she felt his love for her a little bit stronger, a little bit more clearly. It was the type of love she hadn't known before. It was the kind of love that was hard to trust. But she was learning, day by day, to open herself up to that love.

"I know how much I love you, Tyler." She put her hand over his strong, steadily beating heart. "And if you love me even half as much as I love you? I'm a very lucky woman."

\* \* \* \* \*

SHE SIGHED. He was very handsome. She loved the way his eyes crinkled when he smiled. She loved the strong, chiseled lines of his wide mouth, the high cheekbones, the thick black wavy hair around his leonine face. His chest was a work of art in itself. She had to force herself not to look at it too much. It was broad and muscular, under a thick mat of curling black hair that ran down to the waistband of his silk pajamas. Apparently, he didn't like jackets, because he never wore one with the bottoms. His arms were muscular, without being overly so. He would have delighted an artist.

"What are you thinking so hard about?" he wondered aloud.

"That an artist would love painting you," she blurted out, and then flushed then cleared her throat. "Sorry. I wasn't thinking."

He lifted both eyebrows. "Miss Ashton," he scoffed, "you aren't by any chance flirting with me, are you?"

"Mr. Coleman, the thought never crossed my mind!"

"Don't obsess over me," he said firmly, but his eyes were still twinkling. "I'm a married man."

She sighed. "Yes, thank goodness."

His eyebrows lifted in a silent question.

"Well, if you weren't married, I'd probably disgrace myself. Imagine, trying to ravish a sick man in bed because I'm obsessing over the way he looks without a shirt!"

He burst out laughing. "Go away, you bad girl."

Her own eyes twinkled. "I'll banish myself to the kitchen and make lovely things for you to eat."

"I'll look forward to that."

She smiled and left him.

He looked after her with conflicting emotions. He had a wife. Sadly, one who was a disappointment in almost every way; a cold woman who took and took without a thought of giving anything back. He'd married her thinking she was the image of his mother. Elise had seemed very different while they were dating. But the minute the ring was on her finger, she was off on her travels, spending more and more of his money, linking up with old friends whom she paid to travel with her. She was never home. In fact, she made a point of avoiding her husband as much as possible.

This really was the last straw, though, ignoring him when he was ill. It had cut him to the quick to have Todd and Niki see the emptiness of their relationship. He wasn't that sick. It was the principle of the thing. Well, he had some thinking to do when he left the Ashtons, didn't he?

CHRISTMAS DAY WAS BOISTEROUS. Niki and Edna and three other women took turns putting food on the table for an unending succession of people who worked for the Ashtons. Most were cowboys, but several were executives from Todd's oil corporation.

Niki liked them all, but she was especially fond of their children. She dreamed of having a child of her own one day. She spent hours in department stores, ogling the baby things.

She got down on the carpet with the children around the Christmas tree, oohing and aahing over the presents as they opened them. One little girl who was six years old got a Barbie doll with a holiday theme. The child cried when she opened the gaily wrapped package.

"Lisa, what's wrong, baby?" Niki cooed, drawing her into her lap.

"Daddy never buys me dolls, and I love dolls so much, Niki," she whispered. "Thank you!" She kissed Niki and held on tight.

"You should tell him that you like dolls, sweetheart," Niki said, hugging her close.

"I did. He bought me a big yellow truck."

"A what?"

"A truck, Niki," the child said with a very grown-up sigh. "He wanted a little boy. He said so."

Niki looked as indignant as she felt. But she forced herself to smile at the child. "I think little girls are very sweet," she said softly, brushing back the pretty dark hair.

"So do I," Blair said, kneeling down beside them. He smiled at the child, too. "I wish I had a little girl."

"You do? Honest?" Lisa asked, wide-eyed.

"Honest."

She got up from Niki's lap and hugged the big man. "You're nice."

He hugged her back. It surprised him, how much he wanted a child. He drew back, the smile still on his face. "So are you, precious."

"I'm going to show Mama my doll," she said. "Thanks, Niki!"

"You're very welcome."

The little girl ran into the dining room, where the adults were finishing dessert.

"Poor thing," Niki said under her breath. "Even if he thinks it, he shouldn't have told her."

"She's a nice child," he said, getting to his feet. He looked down at Niki. "You're a nice child, yourself."

She made a face at him. "Thanks. I think."

His dark eyes held an expression she'd never seen before. They fell to her waistline and jerked back up. He turned away. "Any more coffee going? I'm sure mine's cold."

"Edna will have made a new pot by now," she said. His attitude disconcerted her. Why had he looked at her that way? Her eyes followed him as he strode back into the dining room, towering over most of the other men. The little girl smiled up at him, and he ruffled her hair.

He wanted children. She could see it. But apparently his wife didn't. What a waste, she thought. What a wife he had. She felt sorry for him. He'd said when he was engaged that he was crazy about Elise. Why didn't she care enough to come when he was ill?

"It's not my business," she told herself firmly.

It wasn't. But she felt very sorry for him just the same. If he'd married *her*, they'd have a houseful of children. She'd take care of him and love him and nurse him when he was sick…she pulled herself up short. He was a married man. She shouldn't be thinking such things.

SHE'D BOUGHT PRESENTS online for her father and Edna and Blair. She was careful to get Blair something impersonal. She didn't want his wife to think she was chasing him or anything. She picked out a tie tac, a *fleur de lis* made of solid gold. She couldn't understand why she'd chosen such a thing. He had Greek ancestry, as far as she knew, not French. It had been an impulse.

Her father had gone to answer the phone, a call from a business associate who wanted to wish him happy holidays, leaving Blair and Niki alone in the living room by the tree. She felt like an idiot for making the purchase.

Now Blair was opening the gift, and she ground her teeth together when he took the lid off the box and stared at it with wide, stunned eyes.

"I'm sorry," she began self-consciously. "The sales slip is in there," she added. "You can exchange it if…"

He looked at her. His expression stopped her tirade midsentence. "My mother was French," he said quietly. "How did you know?"

She faltered. She couldn't manage words. "I didn't. It was an impulse."

His big fingers smoothed over the tie tac. "In fact, I had one just like it that she bought me when I graduated from college." He swallowed. Hard. "Thanks."

"You're very welcome."

His dark eyes pinned hers. "Open yours now."

She fumbled with the small box he'd had hidden in his suitcase until this morning. She tore off the ribbons and opened it. Inside was the most beautiful brooch she'd ever seen. It was a golden orchid on an ivory background. The orchid was purple with a yellow center, made of delicate amethyst and topaz and gold.

She looked at him with wide, soft eyes. "It's so beautiful…"

He smiled with real affection. "It reminded me of you, when I saw it in the jewelry store," he lied, because he'd had it commissioned by a noted jewelry craftsman, just for her. "Little hothouse orchid," he teased.

She flushed. She took the delicate brooch out of its box and pinned it to the bodice of her black velvet dress. "I've never had anything so lovely," she faltered. "Thank you."

He stood up and drew her close to him. "Thank you, Niki." He bent and started to brush her mouth with his, but forced himself to deflect the kiss to her soft cheek. "Merry Christmas."

She felt the embrace to the nails of her toes. He smelled of expensive cologne and soap, and the feel of that powerful body so close to hers made her vibrate inside. She was flustered by the contact, and uneasy because he was married.

She laughed, moving away. "I'll wear it to church every Sunday," she promised without really looking at him.

He cleared his throat. The contact had affected him, too. "I'll wear mine to board meetings, for a lucky charm," he teased gently. "To ward off hostile take-overs."

"I promise it will do the job," she replied, and grinned.

Her father came back to the living room, and the sudden, tense silence was broken. Conversation turned to politics and the weather, and Niki joined in with forced cheerfulness.

But she couldn't stop touching the orchid brooch she'd pinned to her dress.

TIME PASSED. Blair's visits to the ranch had slowed until they were almost nonexistent. Her father said Blair was trying to make his marriage work. Niki thought, privately, that it would take a miracle to turn fun-loving Elise into a housewife. But she forced herself not to dwell on it. Blair was married. Period. She did try to go out more with her friends, but never on a blind date again. The experience with Harvey had affected her more than she'd realized.

Graduation day came all too soon. Niki had enjoyed college. The daily commute was a grind, especially in the harsh winter, but thanks to Tex, who could drive in snow and ice, it was never a problem. Her grade point average was good enough for a magna cum laude award. And she'd already purchased her class ring months before.

"Is Blair coming with Elise, do you think?" Niki asked her father as they parted inside the auditorium just before the graduation ceremony.

He looked uncomfortable. "I don't think so," he said. "They've had some sort of blowup," he added. "Blair's butler, Jameson, called me last night. He said Blair locked himself in his study and won't come out."

"Oh, dear," Niki said, worried. "Can't he find a key and get in?"

"I'll suggest that," he promised. He forced a smile. "Go graduate. You've worked hard for this."

She smiled. "Yes, I have. Now all I have to do is decide if I want to go on to graduate school or get a job."

"A job?" he scoffed. "As if you'll ever need to work."

"You're rich," she pointed out. "I'm not."

"You're rich, too," he argued. He bent and kissed her cheek, a little uncomfortably. He wasn't a demonstrative man. "I'm so proud of you, honey."

"Thanks, Daddy!"

"Don't forget to turn the tassel to the other side when the president hands you your diploma."

"I won't forget."


THE CEREMONY WAS LONG, and the speaker was tedious. By the time he finished, the audience was restless, and Niki just wanted it over with.

She was third in line to get her diploma. She thanked the dean, whipped her tassel to the other side as she walked offstage and grinned to herself, imagining her father's pleased expression.

It took a long time for all the graduates to get through the line, but at last it was over, and Niki was outside with her father, congratulating classmates and working her way to the parking lot.

She noted that, when they were inside the car, her father was frowning.

"I turned my tassel," she reminded him.

He sighed. "Sorry, honey. I was thinking about Blair."

Her heart jumped. "Did you call Jameson?"

"Yes. He finally admitted that Blair hasn't been sober for three days. Apparently, the divorce is final, and Blair found out some unsavory things about his wife."

"Oh, dear." She tried not to feel pleasure that Blair

was free. He'd said often enough that he thought of Niki as a child. "What sort of things?"

"I can't tell you, honey. It's very private stuff."

She drew in a long breath. "We should go get him and bring him to the ranch," she said firmly. "He shouldn't be on his own in that sort of mood."

He smiled softly. "You know, I was just thinking the same thing. Call Dave and have them get the Learjet over here. You can come with me if you like."

"Thanks."

He shrugged. "I might need the help," he mused. "Blair gets a little dangerous when he drinks, but he'd never hit a woman," he added.

She nodded. "Okay."

BLAIR DIDN'T RESPOND to her father's voice asking him to open the door. Muffled curses came through the wood, along with sounds of a big body bumping furniture.

"Let me try," Niki said softly. She rapped on the door. "Blair?" she called.

There was silence, followed by the sound of footsteps coming closer. "Niki?" came a deep, slurred voice.

"Yes, it's me."

He unlocked the door and opened it. He looked terrible. His face was flushed from too much alcohol. His black, wavy hair was ruffled. His blue shirt, unbuttoned and untucked, looking as if he'd slept in it. So did his black pants. He was a little unsteady on his feet. His eyes roved over Niki's face with warm affection.

She reached out and caught his big hand in both of hers. "You're coming home with us," she said gently. "Come on, now."

"Okay," he said, without a single protest.

Jameson, standing to one side, out of sight, sighed with relief. He grinned at her father.

Blair drew in a long breath. "I'm pretty drunk."

"That's okay," Niki said, still holding tight to his hand. "We won't let you drive."

He burst out laughing. "Damned little brat," he muttered.

She grinned at him.

"You dressed up to come visit me?" he asked, looking from her to her father.

"It was my graduation today," Niki said.

Blair grimaced. "Damn! I meant to come. I really did. I even got you a present." He patted his pockets. "Oh, hell, it's in my desk. Just a minute."

He managed to stagger over to the desk without falling. He dredged out a small wrapped gift. "But you can't open it until I'm sober," he said, putting it in her hands.

"Oh. Well, okay," she said. She cocked her head. "Are you planning to have to run me down when I open it, then?"

His eyes twinkled. "Who knows?"

"We'd better go before he changes his mind," her father said blithely.

"I won't," Blair promised. "There's too damned much available liquor here. You only keep cognac and Scotch whiskey," he reminded his friend.

"I've had Edna hide the bottles, though," her father assured him.

"I've had enough anyway."

"Yes, you have. Come on," Niki said, grabbing Blair's big hand in hers.

He followed her like a lamb, not even complaining at

her assertiveness. He didn't notice that Todd and Jameson were both smiling with pure amusement.

WHEN THEY GOT back to Catelow, and the Ashton ranch, Niki led Blair up to the guest room and set him down on the big bed.

"Sleep," she said, "is the best thing for you."

He drew in a ragged breath. "I haven't slept for days," he confessed. "I'm so tired, Niki."

She smoothed back his thick, cool black hair. "You'll get past this," she said with a wisdom far beyond her years. "It only needs time. It's fresh, like a raw wound. You have to heal until it stops hurting so much."

He was enjoying her soft hand in his hair. Too much. He let out a long sigh. "Some days I feel my age."

"You think you're old?" she chided. "We've got a cowhand, Mike, who just turned seventy. Know what he did yesterday? He learned to ride a bicycle."

His eyebrows arched. "Are you making a point?"

"Yes. Age is only in the mind."

He smiled sardonically. "My mind is old, too."

"I'm sorry you couldn't have had children," she lied and felt guilty that she was glad about it. "Sometimes they make a marriage work."

"Sometimes they end it," he retorted.

"Fifty-fifty chance."

"Elise would never have risked her figure to have a child," he said coldly. "She even said so." He grimaced. "We had a hell of a fight after the Christmas I spent here. It disgusted me that she'd go to some party with her friends and not even bother to call to see how I was. She actually said to me the money was nice. It was a pity I came with it."

"I'm so sorry," she said with genuine sympathy. "I can't imagine the sort of woman who'd marry a man for what he had. I couldn't do that, even if I was dirt-poor."

He looked up into soft, pretty gray eyes. "No," he agreed. "You're the sort who'd get down in the mud with your husband and do anything you had to do to help him. Rare, Niki. Like that hothouse orchid pin I gave you for Christmas."

She smiled. "I wear it all the time. It's so beautiful."

"Like you."

She made a face. "I'm not beautiful."

"What's inside you is," he replied, and he wasn't kidding.

She flushed a little. "Thanks."

He drew in a breath and shuddered. "Oh, God…" He shot out of the bed, heading toward the bathroom. He barely made it to the toilet in time. He lost his breakfast and about a fifth of bourbon.

When he finished, his stomach hurt. And there was Niki, with a wet washcloth. She bathed his face, helped him to the sink to wash out his mouth then helped him back to bed.

He couldn't help remembering his mother, his sweet French mother, who'd sacrificed so much for him, who'd cared for him, loved him. It hurt him to remember her. He'd thought Elise resembled her. But it was this young woman, this angel, who was like her.

"Thanks," he managed to croak out.

"You'll be all right," she said. "But just in case, I'm going downstairs right now to hide all the liquor."

There was a lilt in her voice. He lifted the wet cloth he'd put over his eyes and peered up through a growing massive headache. She was smiling. It was like the sun coming out.

"Better hide it good," he teased.

She grinned. "Can I get you anything before I leave?"

"No, honey. I'll be fine."

Honey. Her whole body rippled as he said the word. She tried to hide her reaction to it, but she didn't have the experience for such subterfuge. He saw it and worried. He couldn't afford to let her get too attached to him. He was too old for her. Nothing would change that.

She got up, moving toward the door.

"Niki," he called softly.

She turned.

"Thanks," he said huskily.

She only smiled, before she went out and closed the door behind her.

*Don't miss*
*WYOMING RUGGED by Diana Palmer,*
*available December 2015 wherever*
*Harlequin® HQN books and ebooks are sold.*
*www.Harlequin.com*

# COMING NEXT MONTH FROM

**H** HARLEQUIN®

# SPECIAL EDITION

## Available December 15, 2015

### #2449 Fortune's Secret Heir
*The Fortunes of Texas: All Fortune's Children*
by Allison Leigh
The last thing Ella Thomas expects when she's hired to work a fancy party is to meet Prince Charming...yet that's what she finds in millionaire businessman Ben Robinson. But can the sexy tech mogul open up his heart to find his very own Cinderella?

### #2450 Having the Cowboy's Baby
*Brighton Valley Cowboys*
by Judy Duarte
Country singer Carly Rayburn wants to focus on her promising singing career—so she reluctantly cuts off her affair with sexy cowboy Ian McAllister. But when she discovers she's pregnant with his child, she finds so much more in the arms of the rugged rancher.

### #2451 The Widow's Bachelor Bargain
*The Bachelors of Blackwater Lake*
by Teresa Southwick
When real estate developer Sloan Holden meets beautiful widow Maggie Potter, he does his best to resist his attraction to the single mom. But a family might just be in store for this Blackwater Lake trio...one that only Sloan, Maggie and her daughter can build together!

### #2452 Abby, Get Your Groom!
*The Camdens of Colorado*
by Victoria Pade
Dylan Camden hires Abby Crane to style his sister for her wedding...but his motives aren't pure. To make amends for the Camden clan's past wrongdoings, Dylan must make Abby aware of her past. But what's a bachelor to do when he falls for the very girl he's supposed to help?

### #2453 Three Reasons to Wed
*The Cedar River Cowboys*
by Helen Lacey
Widower Grady Parker isn't looking to replace the wife he's loved and lost. Marissa Ellis is hardly looking for love herself—let alone with the handsome husband of her late best friend. But fate and Grady's three little girls have other ideas!

### #2454 A Marine for His Mom
*Sugar Falls, Idaho*
by Christy Jeffries
When single mom Maxine Walker's young son launches a military pen pal project, she's just glad her child has a male role model in his life. But nobody expected Gunnery Sergeant Matthew Cooper to steal the hearts of everyone in the small town of Sugar Falls, Idaho—especially Maxine's!

---

**YOU CAN FIND MORE INFORMATION ON UPCOMING HARLEQUIN® TITLES, FREE EXCERPTS AND MORE AT WWW.HARLEQUIN.COM.**

HSECNM1215

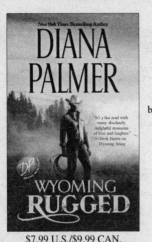

$7.99 U.S./$9.99 CAN.

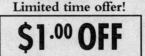

## SPECIAL EXCERPT FROM

### HARLEQUIN

# SPECIAL EDITION

*When tycoon Ben Robinson enlists temp Ella Thomas
to help him uncover Fortune family secrets, will the
closed-off Prince Charming be able to resist the charms
of his beautiful Cinderella?*

*Read on for a sneak preview of*
*FORTUNE'S SECRET HEIR, the first installment in the*
*2016 Fortunes of Texas twentieth anniversary continuity,*
***ALL FORTUNE'S CHILDREN***.

Ben figured it was only a matter of time before the security
guards came to check that he'd exited. But having gotten
what he'd come for, he had no reason to stay.

He went out the door and it closed automatically behind
him. When he tested it out of curiosity, it was locked.

"Crazy old bat," he muttered under his breath.

But he didn't really believe it.

Kate Fortune was many things. Of that he was certain.

But crazy wasn't one of them.

He looked around, getting his bearings before setting
off to his left. It was dark, only a few lights situated here
and there to show off some landscape feature. But he soon
made his way around the side of the enormous house and
to the front, which was not just well lit, but magnificently
so. He stopped at the valet and handed over his ticket to a
skinny kid in a black shirt and trousers.

He tried to imagine Ella dashing off the way this kid
was to retrieve his car, parked somewhere on the vast
property. He couldn't quite picture it.

But in his head, he could picture *her* quite clearly.

Not the red hair. That just reminded him of Stephanie. But the faint gap in her toothy smile and the clear light shining from her pretty eyes.

That was all Ella.

A moment later, when the valet returned with his Porsche, Ben got in and drove away.

*Don't miss*
*FORTUNE'S SECRET HEIR*
*by* New York Times *bestselling author Allison Leigh,*
*available January 2016 wherever*
*Harlequin® Special Edition books and ebooks are sold.*

www.Harlequin.com

# REQUEST YOUR FREE BOOKS!
## 2 FREE NOVELS PLUS 2 FREE GIFTS!

### ⟨H⟩ HARLEQUIN®

# SPECIAL EDITION
## Life, Love & Family

**YES!** Please send me 2 FREE Harlequin® Special Edition novels and my 2 FREE gifts (gifts are worth about $10). After receiving them, if I don't wish to receive any more books, I can return the shipping statement marked "cancel." If I don't cancel, I will receive 6 brand-new novels every month and be billed just $4.74 per book in the U.S. or $5.49 per book in Canada. That's a savings of at least 12% off the cover price! It's quite a bargain! Shipping and handling is just 50¢ per book in the U.S. and 75¢ per book in Canada.* I understand that accepting the 2 free books and gifts places me under no obligation to buy anything. I can always return a shipment and cancel at any time. Even if I never buy another book, the two free books and gifts are mine to keep forever.

235/335 HDN GH3Z

| | |
|---|---|
| Name | (PLEASE PRINT) |

| | |
|---|---|
| Address | Apt. # |

| | | |
|---|---|---|
| City | State/Prov. | Zip/Postal Code |

Signature (if under 18, a parent or guardian must sign)

### Mail to the **Reader Service**:
**IN U.S.A.:** P.O. Box 1867, Buffalo, NY 14240-1867
**IN CANADA:** P.O. Box 609, Fort Erie, Ontario L2A 5X3

**Want to try two free books from another line?**
**Call 1-800-873-8635 or visit www.ReaderService.com.**

* Terms and prices subject to change without notice. Prices do not include applicable taxes. Sales tax applicable in N.Y. Canadian residents will be charged applicable taxes. Offer not valid in Quebec. This offer is limited to one order per household. Not valid for current subscribers to Harlequin Special Edition books. All orders subject to credit approval. Credit or debit balances in a customer's account(s) may be offset by any other outstanding balance owed by or to the customer. Please allow 4 to 6 weeks for delivery. Offer available while quantities last.

**Your Privacy**—The Reader Service is committed to protecting your privacy. Our Privacy Policy is available online at www.ReaderService.com or upon request from the Reader Service.

We make a portion of our mailing list available to reputable third parties that offer products we believe may interest you. If you prefer that we not exchange your name with third parties, or if you wish to clarify or modify your communication preferences, please visit us at www.ReaderService.com/consumerschoice or write to us at Reader Service Preference Service, P.O. Box 9062, Buffalo, NY 14240-9062. Include your complete name and address.

HSE15

# THE WORLD IS BETTER WITH

*Romance*

Harlequin has everything from contemporary, passionate and heartwarming to suspenseful and inspirational stories.

Whatever your mood, we have a romance just for you!

Connect with us to find your next great read, special offers and more.

/HarlequinBooks

@HarlequinBooks

www.HarlequinBlog.com

www.Harlequin.com/Newsletters

**HARLEQUIN®**

A *Romance* FOR EVERY MOOD™

www.Harlequin.com